He took a mouthful of beer. "I'd like a swim myself but..."

"But it wouldn't do to rub shoulders with the workers?"

"Are you accusing me of being a snob?" His arctic tones could have frozen water.

"Aren't you?" She wondered why she wanted to provoke him, knowing how hot-tempered he could be.

He hesitated for a moment. "No, I don't think I'm a snob. In fact," his lips twisted into a sneer, "I enjoy rubbing shoulders with my workers. Some more than others, of course."

Before she realized his intention, he drew her into a darkened corner of the garden. They were shielded from the others by a rose-covered trellis. His mouth came down on hers, hard and angry. It was a punishing kiss, and he crushed her so tightly against him she feared she might suffocate. But—what bliss!

Awards and Commendations

Margaret Tanner has just been voted Author of the Year at Aussie Authors. She also won First Prize a few years ago in a competition organized by the Romance Writers of Australia, for an unpublished full manuscript, and received a "Highly Commended" for her entry in the Clendon (Romance Writers of New Zealand's unpublished full manuscript award). At present she has an unpublished manuscript (*Storm Girl*) in the semi-finals of the Amazon Break Through Novel Award.

Cardinal Sin

by

Margaret Tanner

This is a work of fiction. Names, characters, places, and incidents are either the product of the author's imagination or are used fictitiously, and any resemblance to actual persons living or dead, business establishments, events, or locales, is entirely coincidental.

Cardinal Sin

COPYRIGHT © 2008 by Margaret Tanner

All rights reserved. No part of this book may be used or reproduced in any manner whatsoever without written permission of the author or The Wild Rose Press except in the case of brief quotations embodied in critical articles or reviews.

Contact Information: info@thewildrosepress.com

Cover Art by *Jane Wiedenhoefer*

The Wild Rose Press
PO Box 706
Adams Basin, NY 14410-0706
Visit us at www.thewildrosepress.com

Publishing History
Vintage Rose Edition, 2008
Print ISBN 1-60154-288-7

Published in the United States of America

Dedication

To my friends at
the Melbourne Romance Writers Guild

Chapter 1

Make Love Not War!
Bryce Harrington cursed as an antiwar protester shoved a placard through his car window. Unwashed bloody hippies, disrupting a man going about his lawful business. It was 1966, for God's sake. The government ought to lock up the lot of them.

"No conscripts for Vietnam!" a young woman screamed. Bryce felt tempted to press his foot on the accelerator and scatter them all in his wake. He was going to be late, and he didn't like tardiness. It showed a lack of discipline.

When he arrived at work, he parked the car and climbed out. "Damn it." Some moronic protester had scratched the door of his car.

In his office another shock awaited. He found a note from his secretary.

I'm sorry. Have gone home. Felt a migraine coming on.

He slammed the door of the executive suite and marched down the corridor to see Miss Bumpstead, head of the typing pool. What a shocker of a morning it had been. A bloody nightmare.

The stray puppy he had been feeding for more than a month had been run over by some creep who didn't even have the decency to stop and check on the little mutt's welfare. Just left him lying on the road like a piece of garbage.

After taking the dog to the vet to be put down because the injuries were so severe, he'd got caught up in that antiwar demonstration. And now, to top it off, his secretary had gone home and left him at the mercy of some giggling little girlie from the typing pool.

"Good morning, Miss Bumpstead." Mustering all the willpower he possessed was the only way he managed to keep the anger out of his voice. No point in getting the old dear offside. "I'm sorry to trouble you, but my secretary's gone home sick, and I've several urgent letters to dictate. I'll need to borrow one of your girls."

"Certainly." She jumped to attention like a soldier on parade. "Right away, Mr. Harrington."

"Thank you." He forced a smile, hoping it didn't look like a snarl. She had been employed by the company for years and deserved a bit of respect. He had always followed his father's dictum: "Treat your elders with consideration—they've earned it."

****

Bryce Harrington always looked impressive, tungsten tough. This morning Caroline watched him as he spoke to Miss Bumpstead. Not pretty-boy handsome, but he had a strong, character-filled, no-nonsense face. His full, sensual mouth looked extremely kissable. What would it feel like being held in those strong arms? Having his hot lips pressed against hers? Butterflies fluttered around in the pit of her stomach. His gray eyes held the slightly jaded world-weariness of a man who worked and played hard. Not an ounce of excess fat could be seen on his tall, lean frame.

"Miss Dennison."

Caroline jumped when Miss Bumpstead spoke to her. "You do shorthand, don't you?"

"Y...Yes." Embarrassed heat crept into her cheeks. If this woman could read minds, Caroline Dennison was a dead duck. Thank goodness Miss Bumpstead was focusing most of her attention on Bryce Harrington.

"I'm sure Miss Dennison will be glad to act as your secretary. She's only been here for a few months, but she's a conscientious worker."

"Thank you. Come along, Miss Dennison. I don't mean to rush you, but these letters are urgent."

Caroline stood. The nerves in her stomach knotted, and her throat suddenly felt dry and scratchy. She had dreamed about this moment since joining Harrington and Son, Building Consultants, three months ago as a junior typist. *Get a grip on yourself, girl*, she thought frantically. *You've wanted to be near him. This is your big chance. Don't ruin it now.*

Close up, Bryce looked even more imposing. He

radiated the aura of success and power only supreme self-confidence and enormous wealth could give.

"I...I haven't taken shorthand for a while. My speeds might have dropped." Why did she always feel so inadequate?

His eyes narrowed and he pushed at a dark swathe of hair that kept flopping onto his forehead. He had the type of brown, almost-black hair that would have looked unruly if it wasn't so superbly cut. She felt an overwhelming desire to run her fingers through it. He didn't appear to use very much hair oil, either. Why did so many young men ruin their hair by slathering it with oils or creams?

"I'm sure you'll be fine—Caroline, is it?" He favored her with a wide, white-toothed smile. He was gorgeous.

He strode off, giving her no option but to grab her bag and follow. She didn't know where his office was, the executive office suite being a definite no-go area for lowly typists.

He gave the typing pool door a shove and stood back to allow her to pass through. As their bodies almost touched she was close enough to smell spicy aftershave lotion mingled with his potent, musky male scent before the door slammed behind them and he stormed down the corridor with her scurrying behind him like a mouse chasing after a piece of cheese.

They passed two closed doors. The third he shouldered open. Caroline's heart raced as she nervously entered the inner sanctum. It contained a huge filing cabinet, an office desk with the latest model electric typewriter, and a small switchboard.

"Right. This is your office, Caroline. I'm through here." He gestured to a connecting door that stood half open. "Get your notebook. We need to start immediately. We've got a lot of work to get through."

"I haven't got a notebook."

He gave an exasperated snort. "My secretary keeps hers in the desk, I suppose. Help yourself to anything you need." He turned on his heel and strode back to his office.

With trembling hands, Caroline opened the top drawer of the desk and rummaged around until she found a shorthand notepad and several sharpened pencils. Was she violating the secretary's privacy by going through her desk? Grabbing up a couple of pencils, she made her way to the boss's door. Hesitating for a moment, she took several deep breaths before gathering up enough courage to give a tentative knock.

He wrenched it open. "For heaven's sake, girl, don't dither. We'll be here all night, at this rate."

She followed him into his personal lair, nervously glancing around as she did so. A huge desk in the center of the room dominated the area. He threw himself into a brown leather chair positioned under a large window, while she hovered in front of him.

"Sit down, I don't bite." His lips tightened as she sat opposite and opened her notebook, pencil poised, ready to start. He looked as if he were at the end of his tether.

"All my letters commence and finish the same way, so you can take the body of the letter and fill in the rest later."

He started dictating, his voice clear, well modulated. At first it proved an easy task to take down what he said, even though her fingers trembled. *Don't let nerves turn you into a gibbering idiot.* Once he got into his rhythm, however, his tempo quickened, causing her to get flustered.

"I'm sorry, Mr. Harrington, but I missed the last few words."

He frowned. "Read me back the last couple of lines."

"We are interested in opening up..."

"Wrong, wrong." He took a couple of deep breaths. "Sorry for snapping. It should read: We are interested in taking up an option on the parcel of land near the golf course, provided we can get government planning approval. Got it?" He started dictating again, scarcely pausing for breath.

Caroline's pencil flew across the page. Her outlines were so hurried she would have trouble transcribing them later on. Just when she felt as if her hand might drop off, he finished.

"That's it. How long will it take you to type them up?" He glanced at his watch. "It's two o'clock now."

"I'm not sure."

"I have to be out of here no later than five-thirty. I

have a dinner engagement. Do the best you can. I'll sign the ones you've finished before I go." He gave one of his fabulous smiles and she nearly melted into a puddle at his feet. "Leave any others in my inbox, and I'll deal with them first thing in the morning. Oh, original and two carbon copies, please."

Caroline returned to the secretary's office and searched through the drawers until she found some headed paper with *Harrington Constructions* printed across the top in black raised lettering. Inserting the paper and two carbon copies as instructed, she commenced typing. What a dream this electric machine was to use! Much better than the old manual blunderbusses provided for them in the typing pool.

She disciplined herself to type carefully and steadily. It would be quicker in the end. All the letters were signed "Bryce A. Harrington, Managing Director." She wondered what the A stood for. Alexander, most probably, because that was Harrington Senior's name.

She had chanced a glance at her boss from time to time as he dictated. His skin was deeply tanned, as if he spent a lot of time at the beach. When he walked he did so with a lithe, feline grace that only added to his already lethal magnetism.

She would never forget the breathtaking smile he had given her in the elevator on her first day at work, three months ago.

On her second day at work, an elderly woman had fallen in the street. Before she could rush over and assist, Bryce was already there. He helped the old lady to her feet, then bent down to gather up the contents of her handbag. Numerous items had been strewn all over the street, and as he picked them up a passerby nearly trod on his hand.

Unperturbed, he collected every item, even a lipstick that had rolled into the gutter, put them back into the bag and handed it back to the lady. Accepting her thanks with a smile, he waved down a taxi, helped her into it and gave the driver a twenty-dollar note. It was all done with a minimum of fuss and an easygoing charm. Caroline was immediately smitten.

Now, after seeing him intermittently over the past

few weeks and being on the receiving end of his lethal smile, she was more than smitten. She had committed the cardinal sin of falling in love with the "big boss"—the omnipotent Bryce Harrington. The only son and heir of a millionaire society family was out of her league. Her brain told her this, but her poor, foolish heart refused to listen.

She typed on resolutely until her head started throbbing and her fingers kept slipping off the keyboard. If only she had time to get a nice, hot cup of tea. At exactly fifteen minutes past five, Bryce swept in.

"Have you finished yet?"

He had to be joking. No secretary on the planet could type that fast.

"Those are." She pointed to a neat pile of letters.

"Thanks." He picked them up and cast a cursory eye over them. "They look okay, but I won't know until I check them more thoroughly. You'll hear soon enough if they aren't." He gave a half smile, half grimace, and it emphasized a dimple in his chin. "I can be a hard taskmaster."

What an understatement. According to office gossip, he demanded perfection and would settle for nothing less.

"Mr. Harrington?"

"Yes?" He quirked an eyebrow.

"I'm going to be here for another couple of hours, at least. What do I do about a meal?"

"You can worry about that later." His office door closed with a loud click.

Caroline seethed as she continued typing. Surely he didn't expect her to stay late without a break. At five-thirty he came out again and started towards the door.

"Were the letters all right?"

"Yes, thanks." His reply was crisp and sharp as a frosty morning. He looked agitated. Something must be irritating him.

"The kitchen is across the passageway," he continued. "You're welcome to use it. Joan, my secretary, keeps a good supply of coffee and biscuits. Take some money out of petty cash and buy yourself a hamburger or something on the way home if you have to stay too late. Oh, and make sure you catch a cab home. There should be a book of travel vouchers in Joan's desk."

After another hour of typing, the words started to blur, so Caroline took a break and found the small, well-appointed kitchen with the latest stainless steel appliances.

Making herself a cup of tea, using a plain cup and saucer, she squashed down the almost overwhelming urge to use the VIP fine bone china, in case she dropped it. The secretary obviously organized refreshments when required.

In the refrigerator she found a bottle of milk, some butter, and several bottles of expensive wine. Jars of oysters, tiny savory onions, and assorted snacks graced the shelves. Nothing but the best for any Harrington visitors.

She helped herself to a couple of biscuits and sat on a wooden chair with her arm resting against the sink. She chewed a bite of biscuit thoughtfully. Bryce Harrington's private secretary. It did have a certain ring to it. After rinsing her cup and putting it away, she went back to work.

Just before seven o'clock she pulled the last letter out of the typewriter. Finished, thank goodness! Grabbing up the letters, she put them into the inbox, turned the typewriter off, and prepared to leave.

A full-length mirror hung on the back of the door, but she didn't bother going over to it, just took out her powder compact to apply some fresh lipstick. She looked so ordinary. Nondescript, her mother had always said. Had she been glamorous, maybe Bryce Harrington would have given her more than a cursory, disinterested glance.

She didn't ring for a cab, as it was only a short bus ride home to the small apartment she shared with her girlfriend, Kerry. As she sat on the bus, she glanced at a paper being read by the businessman sitting opposite. Her heart lurched and ice-cold fear almost froze the blood in her veins. The devastating headlines read: "Heavy casualties in Vietnam. On the eighteenth of August, eighteen Australian soldiers from Delta Company of the 6th Royal Australian Regiment were killed in the battle for Long Tan."

Her hands started trembling, and she had to sit on them so the other passengers wouldn't notice.

Fear was like a ton weight pressing down on her lungs, as if she were drowning, only there wasn't any water. Andy was nearly finished at officer training school. Would he be sent to Vietnam to fight? War had killed her father and turned her mother into a bitter woman. She didn't want it claiming her brother, as well.

****

When Caroline reported to the typing pool for work the next morning, Miss Bumpstead marched up to her. Rumor had it she used to be a sergeant major in the army. She certainly looked the part, the hard-faced old battleaxe.

"Oh, there you are." Her look said *about time, too,* even though Caroline had arrived ten minutes early. "You're required in Mr. Harrington's office immediately. His secretary is still indisposed, so he wants you to take her place." She sniffed.

"Me?" Caroline squeaked.

"Yes. See you don't let me down. Your behavior will reflect on me, too. I have a reputation to maintain."

"Poor you." Judith, one of the other typists, commiserated with Caroline.

"Now look here, my girl," Miss Bumpstead reprimanded. "Typists do not make disparaging remarks about Mr. Harrington."

"I'd better be off." Caroline was desperate to escape one of Miss Bumpstead's sanctimonious lectures. Giving Judith a grin, she scurried out of the typing pool. Hopefully for good, she thought, though not wishing Joan any ill.

When she got to her office—*her* office...that sounded great—she gave a gleeful skip. This was definitely a promotion, even if it did prove to be only temporary.

She switched on the typewriter, all the while debating whether it would be the correct procedure to go in and greet her new boss, perhaps offer him coffee? It would be rude if she didn't. On the other hand...

The ringing of the internal phone interrupted her and she picked it up.

"Good morning, Miss Dennison. Could you make a pot of coffee and bring it in to me. Two cups, please."

"Yes, Mr. Harrington, of course."

Two cups? He wasn't alone. She went into the kitchen and set up a tray with a coffeepot, milk, sugar, and a plate of fancy biscuits.

When it was ready, she took it back to the office, tapped on his door and walked in. Oh, God, if only she hadn't. He held a gorgeous redhead in his arms.

"Bryce, darling—" A husky female voice was silenced by his enticing, sexy mouth. Jealousy corroded the lining of Caroline's stomach, paring it away until she felt raw and bleeding.

She cleared her throat. "Mr. Harrington? Y...Your coffee."

He dragged his mouth free, keeping the woman's body close to his own with a hand on her neat little backside.

"Don't you believe in knocking?" His gunmetal gray eyes impaled Caroline, and like a mesmerized rabbit she couldn't look away.

"I did knock, but I guess you..." She nearly said, *Were too preoccupied.* "Um, didn't hear me."

"Put it over there." He waved a tanned, well-manicured hand towards the antique mahogany desk. "Thanks. Well, don't just stand there dithering, I've left plenty of work on your desk."

Did he really think she wanted to stand there watching as he held his lady friend in a passionate clinch?

"Bryce, darling, don't be such a grouch." The redhead gave a breathy laugh. "You'll frighten the poor girl to death."

Caroline pivoted on one stiletto heel—luckily, it didn't snap off—and stifled a sudden jealous impulse to kick the door shut on her way out.

Served her right for committing the cardinal sin, the definite no-no for any sensible secretary—falling in love with the boss. Could she put up with watching him canoodling with other women?

Twenty minutes later, the ravishing redhead glided out. Shereen St. Clair was a top model, elegant, sophisticated, and pencil-thin. Caroline remembered seeing her pictures in the newspapers and fashion magazines. How could any ordinary mortal hope to compete with such perfection?

Chapter 2

Over the next few weeks, Caroline became all too familiar with Bryce Harrington's lady friends. Joan had not returned to work but sent in a letter of resignation. Maybe she had gotten tired of his mercurial mood swings and the continual stream of tantrum-throwing women. Caroline wondered why she herself had consented to constant heartache by accepting the position as his secretary. The rise in salary was welcome, but she earned every cent of it.

She arranged flowers for his current favorite, organized theatre and restaurant bookings, vetted all his calls. Those who had his interest she put through to him, or pacified them if he couldn't come to the phone.

The castoffs? She dealt with them, also. It wasn't easy. Petulant, spoiled socialites or movie stars didn't like being unceremoniously dumped.

As she typed, she stabbed the keys in angry frustration. She shouldn't put up with his bad temper and playboy ways, but she couldn't bear not to see him, either. On the rare occasions when he did smile at her, the whole office lit up like a Christmas tree. He paid her well and was a generous benefactor to several charities. She often sent off six-figure checks, his only stipulation to the recipients being that his donations should remain confidential.

He didn't know how she felt about him, thank goodness. That would be the ultimate humiliation. She longed to be something more than a capable pair of hands and a polite mouthpiece but knew it was an impossible dream. Pigs would fly to the moon before Bryce Harrington took any romantic interest in Caroline Dennison, with her light brown, not-quite-blonde flyaway hair and serviceable chain-store clothes.

The door of his office swung open and Shereen glided out again. She was a striking woman, her slender figure encased in slinky, skin-tight slacks. The matching camisole top displayed gold trim around the neckline and sleeves. She lifted her hand in a desultory salute before tottering off in her ridiculously high gold stilettos, a trail of cloying perfume wafting in her wake.

The phone on her desk rang. "Good afternoon, Mr. Harrington's office, may I help you?"

"Alexander Harrington here. Put me through to my son, would you, please?" Though Harrington Senior sounded authoritative, he was always polite and friendly.

She switched the call through to Bryce's office and continued typing. A few seconds later he stormed out, his face taut with anger.

"Get me that file on the Mountainside estate, please, and I want to see Geoff Davies in here, straight away."

He slammed the communicating door shut. Once again he was in a foul mood.

She put through a call to Mr. Davies' secretary.

"Hi Dulcie, it's Caroline. The boss wants to see Mr. Davies."

"Another drama?" Dulcie chuckled. "I'll tell him. Why do you put up with Harrington?"

"The money's good." What a pathetic lie. She knew perfectly well why she put up with his mood swings, but on pain of death she would never admit it.

****

Mr. Davies smiled as he walked into her office. "How are you, Caroline?" He was the company's senior architect, the one who took charge in Bryce's absence.

"I'm fine, how are you?"

"Not bad, for an old codger. Do you know what the boss wants?"

"No, other than you and the Mountainside files." She handed them over, and Mr. Davies entered Bryce's office without knocking.

The buzzer on her desk sounded about five minutes later. She grabbed her notebook and pencil in case she might need them.

As she walked into Bryce's office, she heard him snarl, "The information has been leaked."

"I didn't mention it to anyone," Mr. Davies protested.

"Then who did? You and I were the only ones to see

those plans and specifications, except..." Bryce shot out of his chair. "What about you, Miss Dennison?"

"I didn't mention it to anyone. I never discuss my work once I leave the office."

"Someone did. Geoff's worked here for years, and I certainly didn't do it." He glared at her. "How much money did they offer you?"

"I didn't do it," she whispered. For Bryce to think her capable of such disloyalty nearly killed her, after the way she had worked and slaved for him over the last few weeks.

"If she says she didn't do it, I believe her." Mr. Davies leapt to her defense. "Don't upset yourself, Caroline."

"Someone leaked that information," Bryce growled. "The land will cost us a fortune now." He slammed his fist so hard on the desk Caroline jumped.

"Those plans were on your desk for the last couple of days, Mr. Harrington." Caroline fought to retain her composure.

"So what?" He took an angry puff on his cigarette. "Someone let the cat out of the bag. God knows what other information has been leaked. With government defense contracts coming up for tender, a security breach like this could jeopardize our chances."

"Miss Francis spent time alone in your office last week."

His face darkened with temper. "Are you insinuating Miss Francis would tamper with my files?"

"If they were open on your desk, she might have seen them. Perhaps she accidentally let something slip. She spent about fifteen minutes in here on Wednesday. Remember? You were called away and told her to wait."

"She could have, granted." He stroked his chin with one long, slender finger. "She was here on her own. But why would she steal them? She doesn't need the money."

"Meaning I do? If you don't feel I'm trustworthy, I'll tender my resignation right now." Caroline made the offer recklessly. "I don't dabble in industrial espionage or whatever it's called."

"You're a bloody fool," she heard Mr. Davies say as she turned and headed towards the door.

"Why would Marilyn do it? "

"You dumped her, Bryce. Ever heard of a woman scorned?" Those were the last words Caroline heard as she fled the office.

****

Once he started to calm down, Bryce realized Davies could be right. A woman scorned. An old-fashioned way of putting it, perhaps, but Marilyn could be a bitch. The more he thought about the idea, the more convinced he became that she had disclosed the information to their competitors out of sheer spite.

What a hell of a day. He massaged the tense muscles in the back of his neck and decided to go home early. He pressed the buzzer, but Caroline didn't answer, so he put his finger back on it and let it rest there. Where was the girl? Cursing to himself, he got to his feet and strode out into her office. Empty.

She had threatened to resign. Surely she wouldn't just walk out and leave him in the lurch. His heart dropped to his boots. When he noticed her bag on the floor beside the desk, he heaved a sigh of relief. If he had to break in another new secretary, it would be the absolute end. Didn't he have enough on his mind?

He sat in the typist's swivel chair. Damn it. She had proved to be an excellent secretary. Pleasant, attractive, with the most amazing blue eyes, and that soft flyaway blonde hair of hers made him itch to run his fingers through it. How she put up with his foul moods, he didn't know.

Even as a child he had been hot-tempered, but of late he exploded with little provocation. Wincing, he recalled some of the things he'd said to her. He shouldn't have accused her of industrial espionage without a shred of evidence. He needed a holiday—that was obvious.

His usual activities left him bored senseless. He even dreaded going to his parents' home tonight for his mother's birthday. A quiet family dinner with just the three of them. He knew what would follow the meal. It happened every time he visited them.

Stalking back into his office, Bryce realized he would have to apologize to Caroline. Hell, he wasn't used to saying "Sorry" to anyone. If it came to losing Caroline or apologizing, well, he knew which was the lesser of the two evils.

Purposely he left the connecting door open, so the moment she returned he heard her.

"Caroline." He leaned into her office from the doorway. "I'd like to speak to you for a moment."

She glanced up and he was shocked to see tear marks on her cheek.

"I owe you an apology." It came out stiffly, but he couldn't help it.

When he saw how pale she looked, he felt like an utter heel, and staring into her shattered blue eyes caused his heart to give a strange, painful lurch.

"I'm sorry about losing my temper before. I hope you'll reconsider. I need you."

Her tremulous lips parted. "I would like to continue working for you, but not if you don't trust me."

"I'm sorry, and apologizing doesn't come easily to me. I do trust you to maintain the confidentiality of our work here. You're a good secretary, one of the best, and I don't want to lose you."

"All right, I'll stay."

"Good. I'm off now. I have a dinner engagement." He started towards the door. "You might as well leave, too. It's after five."

"Thanks, but it doesn't matter."

"There isn't much for you to do here, so you might as well go. Where do you live?" he asked.

"Prahran."

"I'll give you a lift. I'm driving to South Yarra."

"Thank you, but I can catch the bus."

"I said I'd give you a lift."

He waited while she turned the typewriter off and put everything away in the drawer. As she bent to pick up her handbag, he noticed her slim legs. They seemed to go on forever. She wore a mini skirt, but it was only a couple of inches above her knee. Not like some women, who wore skirts so short that when they bent over a man felt compelled to turn his head away as a matter of decency.

For the first time, he studied her. Her face, although not classically beautiful, was fine-boned, with milky white, flawless skin. Her eyes were her best feature, a real forget-me-not blue, round as saucers. A man could drown in them. He couldn't help wondering about her. She walked with the grace of a ballerina, her voice sounded well modulated, and she was articulate. Caroline Dennison was one classy lady.

If she hadn't been his secretary, he would have been tempted to ask her out on a date. She intrigued him, stirred his senses more than any other woman he could remember, but he never mixed business with pleasure. It could prove a potentially explosive combination. He didn't want to run the risk of having it blow up in his face. Caroline would be high maintenance, too. She would expect not only physical but emotional commitment from a man, and he wasn't capable of giving that much of himself to anyone.

"Whereabouts in Prahran do you live?" he asked, as he opened the elevator door and she ducked under his arm.

"Off Commercial Road. I share an apartment with my girlfriend." She gave him the address.

He pressed the ground floor button, and they stood together without speaking. Midway between the second and third floors, the elevator gave a shudder and threw her against him. Bryce caught the faint, elusive perfume of her skin and hair. Roses, perhaps? It smelled sweet, just like her. Her body felt soft, pliant against his. He tightened his arms around her and held her a little longer than necessary.

Then he put her away and stepped back a couple of paces. Taking out his cigarettes, he offered her one.

"No, thanks. I don't smoke."

He flicked a gold lighter, put it to the tip of his cigarette and inhaled deeply. "Filthy habit, but I enjoy it." He grinned. "I don't have many vices."

In the executive car park, Bryce guided her towards a burgundy Jaguar. He opened the passenger side door for her, waited silently while she got in, then closed the door and went around to the driver's side and got in.

Caroline snuggled into the soft leather seats, forcing herself not to ooh and ah at this unaccustomed luxury. From the corner of her eye she watched his well-kept hands on the steering wheel. There were tufts of fine black hair on his fingers. Through lowered lashes she glanced at his profile. His obstinate jaw denoted a determination he didn't try to hide. He had tanned healthy skin, and a well-shaped mouth.

What bliss, being so close to him in the intimate confines of his luxury car. She felt like royalty. A pity she didn't live a hundred miles away.

"Turn here." She directed him from Commercial Road into her street, pointing out the red brick, double-storied house that had been divided into four separate apartments. The lawns were well tended, but the building itself needed updating. She lived in the shadows of multi-storied apartment blocks, and she watched him give it a cursory glance. A man like Bryce Harrington would deem this a slum.

"Thanks for the lift."

"My pleasure." He leaned across and opened the car door for her. "Have a nice evening, and thanks for all the hard work you've done for me." His devastating heart-stopper of a smile nearly caused her to tumble rather than step out of the car.

Caroline entered the small ground-floor apartment she shared with her friend, Kerry Robinson. It wasn't much, just a bedroom, kitchenette, lounge room and bathroom.

Kicking off her shoes, Caroline laid her bag on the dressing table in her bedroom but didn't bother changing out of her work clothes. With the ink that had gotten smeared on her sleeve when she'd put in a new typewriter ribbon, her outfit was due for the laundry anyway.

She padded out to the kitchenette in her stocking feet and began peeling some vegetables for their dinner, to go with the two steaks thawing on the sink.

Just before six o'clock, Kerry breezed in. She flung her bag down on the sink and raked her fingers through her short black hair. "Hi! How did your day go with Mr. High-and-Mighty?"

"All right." Caroline put the steaks in the pan. "He drove me home in his Jaguar."

"Drove you home? Yeah? How come?"

Caroline explained what happened.

"I might have guessed it would be something like that. He's never offered to drive you home before. He's smart enough to realize no other secretary would put up with the crap he dishes out to you. I still say you should leave and get a job somewhere else."

"I know, but..."

"You're breaking your heart over him for nothing. There's no way he's going to notice you, even if you are his secretary." Kerry stabbed the air with her forefinger. "You, of all people, know the type of women he associates with and the reputation he's got. Not a week goes by without him adorning the social pages with some model or actress fawning all over him."

"I know. It's hopeless." Caroline closed her eyes to block out the searing pain of unrequited love. Today in the elevator she had been so close to him, her cheek resting on his chest, her nostrils infused with his scent. "I can't help it. I love him. Just seeing him is better than nothing." Not seeing him would be purgatory.

"Rubbish. If you left and got another job, in time you'd forget all about him. You should be going out with other guys, not wasting your time mooning over someone as unobtainable as he is."

"Everything is cooked. Will I dish up now?" Caroline asked, trying to divert her friend from one of the two topics on which they would never agree. The other was Vietnam. Kerry belonged to several antiwar organizations.

"I'm going to a meeting with Trevor tonight. It's being organized by some mothers from the 'Save our Sons' movement. Why don't you come with us?"

"No, thanks. I'll have an early night."

Caroline liked Trevor. He and Kerry were soulmates, but he was a passionate anti-conscription advocate. With Andy being in the army, she would feel like a traitor if she attended these anti-military rallies.

****

Bryce drove to an exclusive South Yarra street, where he parked his car in the underground car park of his apartment building and caught the elevator up to the top floor. From the elevator he strode along the thickly carpeted corridor to his apartment and, once inside, looked around with a grimace. In one of his weaker moments he had let his girlfriend at the time, an interior designer, decorate for him. It had cost him a small fortune, not that money mattered. The problem was, he wasn't impressed with the décor but couldn't be bothered with the hassles of changing it.

Loosening his tie and shrugging off his jacket, he stepped into his bedroom with its white shag pile carpet. The deep-blue, velvet drapes at the floor-to-ceiling windows and the matching quilt on his king-sized bed did nothing for him. Women would like it, he supposed. Not that any female had ever stayed here. Dinner was the most he ever offered them, and that was only rarely. He was a selfish bastard—he valued his privacy too much.

He slid back the curtains and stared out past the Juliet-type balcony. This was his favorite place, and he guarded this treasure like a miser with a pile of coins—an almost uninterrupted view of the Melbourne skyline. Would he be able to see Prahran from here? Damn it, he wasn't interested in Prahran, and he sure as hell wasn't interested in Caroline Dennison.

As he ran a hand across his jaw and chin, he realized he needed not only a shower but a shave. His bathroom was immaculate, as usual, just like the rest of his apartment. He couldn't bear to live with untidiness and clutter. He was extremely satisfied with the housekeeper who came in daily. She lived in one of the ground floor apartments and would come up at short notice and prepare his evening meal if he required it. Of course, he paid top dollar for her services, but it was worth it.

Strange how he still missed his little stray mutt. No dogs were allowed in the apartment block, but he had built a kennel in the back garden and fed the puppy morning and night. On several occasions he had seen the woman from Apartment Four sneaking food to it, as well, so he wasn't the only sucker.

He changed into a dark navy suit with a pale blue, open-necked shirt. His parents always liked him to dress formally for dinner, but just to be perverse he decided to take a more casual approach. What the hell was wrong with him? His mother's continual nagging had never made him feel this irritable and jittery before.

Right on six o'clock, he left for his parents' home. The streets were crowded with shoppers. The stores were staying open late on Thursdays as well as Fridays in the lead-up to the Christmas shopping frenzy. *What a materialistic farce,* he thought, slamming on the brakes to avoid a couple of hippies who shot out onto the road waving a placard with "No conscripts for Vietnam" scrawled across it in red paint. He couldn't even tell whether they were male or female. Didn't those feral peaceniks ever give up?

It didn't take long to drive to his parents' home, which sprawled amidst park-like gardens in Toorak. The two-storied Victorian mansion was set behind a high bluestone fence. A verandah running across the front was trimmed with fancy iron lacework. The house had been in the Harrington family for three generations, and as an adult he always took a moment to admire it.

He drove through the massive iron gates, which were electronically controlled and glided shut behind him. As he drove up the curved driveway, he inhaled the perfume from the profusely flowering rose bushes lining the driveway. Native and ornamental shrubs were scattered throughout the carefully manicured lawns.

He parked the car out in front, walked to the front door and banged the brass knocker. Easier than using his key. The uniformed housekeeper instantly opened it.

"Good evening, Mr. Harrington. Your mother has been waiting for you."

"How are you, Mrs. Ferguson? Sorry I'm late, but I got held up at work." He followed her through a columned archway and down the carpeted hallway.

His mother sat on a rosewood Regency chair. He had a good eye for antiques, and this was a fine example. The house contained Regency and Hepplewhite furniture that had belonged to the Harrington family for generations.

"Bryce, darling." She rose to greet him with the elegance of a woman half her age.

"Hello, Mother. Happy birthday." He kissed her cool, powdered cheek.

"Ah, there you are, son. We've been waiting for you."

Hello, Dad. Sorry I'm late." He mouthed the polite platitudes that were expected of him.

"Have a drink, son."

"Thanks." He sat down on another of the Regency

chairs to sip his drink. The old man didn't look too bad for his age. His hair was completely gray now, but he still had plenty of it. Thank goodness, baldness didn't run in the family.

"Now, what happened about this Mountainside file? We stand to lose half a million dollars on this deal now." Of course his father would start on him straight away. This was going to be the night from hell.

"I'm not sure how the information leaked out, but I've got my suspicions." He proceeded to tell his father about Marilyn Francis. "You know how vindictive she can be. Turned very nasty when I broke off with her."

"I don't know why you bother with such vulgar types," his mother chipped in, disapproval in her eyes.

"They do have their uses," he drawled, just to irritate her. He had never noticed before how cold and haughty she was. Caroline was soft…

"Don't be so common and crude. You should be thinking of marriage and settling down." She warmed to her theme. "You've had plenty of time to sow your wild oats."

Bryce scowled, knowing what he would hear next. Almost word for word he knew what his father was getting ready to say.

"My sentiments exactly, dear." He took his unlit cigar out of his mouth. "You must think of marrying and producing an heir. After all, once I'm gone, you'll be the last of the Harringtons. What will become of the firm? It's up to you to continue the line. A man doesn't want to see a lifetime of work and ambition go down the drain."

"I've told you before." Bryce tried to keep his temper in check. "I don't intend to marry, at least not yet. Why didn't you have more than one child? Then you wouldn't have to force me to do something I don't want."

"Now, I won't have you speaking in such a disparaging fashion." His mother rose, her lips thin and angry. "I did my duty by your father and gave him a son. Now it's up to you to continue the line. Lady Fontain's daughter, Ashley, is a wonderful girl. You could do worse."

"That empty-headed bimbo? You've got to be kidding."

"They're wealthy people. She has relations high up in

government. Think what they could do for the firm, especially with these defense contracts coming up. You're thirty-four. Your father and I were married before we were thirty."

"More fool you," he snapped. "Isn't dinner ready yet? I'm hungry." What a downright lie. He had lost his appetite. If the arguing continued much longer he would have to get up and leave, before his temper got the better of him and he said something he would later regret.

Like a magic genie Mrs. Ferguson appeared, saving the situation with her announcement that dinner was served. Alexander took his wife's arm and, followed by a still scowling Bryce, they adjourned to the dining room.

The rosewood Regency table was covered with a hand-embroidered lace tablecloth and set with silver cutlery. Anyone would think his mother was entertaining royalty. Bloody ridiculous.

Mrs. Ferguson served the scallop bisque from a Crown Derby soup tureen and, after a whiff of the aroma, Bryce found his appetite returning. One thing for sure, his parents picked the best domestic staff money could buy. A crown roast, with baked vegetables, cauliflower in white sauce, peas and beans followed the soup. Dessert turned out to be his favorite, chocolate brandy soufflé.

They retired to the sitting room to drink their coffee.

"Mother, I forgot to give you your birthday present." He pulled out a small, carefully wrapped package and handed it over.

"Thank you." She kissed his cheek and then undid the ribbon and unwrapped the present. She lifted the lid of the small jeweler's box to display a daisy-shaped ring, a black opal center surrounded by petals of rolled gold.

"Darling, it's beautiful."

He watched her slip it onto the ring finger of her right hand. If there was one thing his mother had a weakness for, it was rings. He thought cynically of the dozens of expensive diamonds locked in the safe upstairs, but felt pleased that she appeared happy with the opal.

It had been Caroline's idea.

"Black opals are lovely. If she doesn't have many opals it should be perfect," she had said.

"Actually, my secretary picked it out for you." Bryce

smiled at his mother, mellowed by fine food and wine.

"Did she? I must say she showed excellent taste."

"What's her name?" his father asked. "She's got such a pleasant voice. A change to hear a well spoken, polite girl these days."

"Naturally she's polite," Bryce snapped. He didn't know why, but thinking about Caroline made him edgy. Guilty conscience for the way he treated her? Because he found himself attracted to her? He ruthlessly squashed the dangerous thought. Hell, he didn't want to go down that route. "Her name is Caroline Dennison."

"Dennison? Does she come from around here?"

Bryce shrugged. "She shares an apartment in Prahran. I don't know anything else about her."

"Dennison." Alexander repeated the name. "I've got a good memory for names. Dennison rings a bell somewhere."

Bryce lit a cigarette and smoked it thoughtfully. "I know nothing about her private life. She's an efficient secretary, which is all I care about. She doesn't come from around here or move in our set. Maybe you conducted some business deal with a Dennison."

"It's an unusual name. No, I'm certain it has nothing to do with business. Oh, well, it will come to me sometime or other, I expect." Shrugging, the older man took out a cigar and started peeling off the wrapper.

"I might push off now." Bryce climbed to his feet.

"Darling, you're not leaving already?"

"Sorry, but I've got an early start in the morning."

"I wanted to discuss the idea of having a small dinner party. We could ask the—"

"No. I know your little schemes, and if you fancy trying your hand at matchmaking again, forget it. By the way, Dad," he said, changing the subject. "Are we having the staff Christmas party here again this year?"

"Yes, our poolside barbecue always goes down well. I see no reason to change it," Alexander said, smiling his satisfaction.

"I don't know why you bother having all those people traipsing through our gardens. After all, they're only workers."

"Now, my dear, they might only be workers as far as

you're concerned, but I've always found it pays dividends to treat employees well," Alexander admonished his wife.

"Well, I'm off," Bryce said.

"Think about Ashley," his mother fired off as a parting shot.

He clamped his teeth together so as not tell her exactly what he did think of Ashley: a selfish, conniving little brat.

Giving his parents a final wave, he left the room. On soundless feet, Mrs. Ferguson appeared to see him out.

His hand clenched into an angry fist in his pocket. His snobbish mother was always trying to push him into matrimony with one or another of the daughters of her socialite friends. His bachelor life suited him admirably. He didn't intend changing it, just to fit in with his mother's plans and aspirations. Why limit yourself to one book when you could have a whole library?

Chapter 3

The alarm rang at seven o'clock. Both Kerry and Caroline yawned and snuggled back under the blankets for an extra few minutes' lie-in, but Caroline got up first, pulling the blankets off her friend as she passed by. She headed for the shower, following their usual routine. Last out of bed started breakfast while the other one used the bathroom.

When Caroline had finished showering, she dressed in a white pleated skirt with a matching short-sleeved top and a navy blue, double-breasted blazer. In November the weather could be unpredictable. It might be cool in the morning but warm up as the day progressed. If it got hot she could discard the blazer. She brushed her hair, then applied some blue eye shadow and a touch of pink lipstick.

Hurrying out to the kitchen, she just managed to rescue the toast before it turned into charcoal. Kerry was reading a magazine instead of watching their breakfast. They only had toast and tea, as there wasn't enough time in their hectic schedule for anything else.

Kerry was lucky to have been issued a work uniform, Caroline thought enviously as they made their way to the bus stop. Pity Harringtons didn't supply uniforms, as well. It was hard trying to dress well besides pay her rent and other expenses, even though she earned good money now that Bryce had given her a raise.

The bus lumbered to a halt. They climbed aboard and found a seat. Caroline only went six stops, whereas Kerry continued on into the central business district.

Harrington Constructions owned the multi-storied building, although they only occupied a couple of floors. Bryce had considerable money independent of his wealthy father. The rumor mill suggested Bryce dabbled in real estate and owned extensive vineyards in the Barossa Valley in South Australia. She'd discovered by accident one day that he owned several prestigious apartment blocks around Melbourne, also.

She caught the elevator up to the fifth floor without seeing anyone. Once in her office she sat down, removed the cover from her typewriter and switched it on. There was nothing left to be typed, so she tidied her desk drawers while waiting for Bryce to arrive.

She always thought of him as Bryce but called him Mr. Harrington if she spoke of or to him. She closed her eyes and let her mind drift. She had overheard him describe her as *mousy* once.

Mousy? He might just as well have said *ugly*. "A plain little nobody" had been her mother's hurtful description. While she denigrated Caroline, her maternal pride had overflowed for Andy. He could do no wrong in her eyes. Fortunately, he hadn't turned out spiteful like their mother.

Caroline had shed a few tears about her mother's unflattering comments, but she had wept bucketfuls over Bryce's description of her. It couldn't stop the way she felt about him, though. Her reward for enduring this? Seeing him every day. How pathetic, like an affection-starved puppy content to accept a pat on the head from its master every now and again. On rare occasions he could be exceedingly charming—when he smiled, wow, he looked like a movie star.

"I don't pay you to daydream."

She shot back to the present to find Bryce hovering over her, an angry glint in his eye.

"I'm sorry. I was waiting for you to come in and give me some work."

No "Good morning, Caroline," just a caustic comment designed to make her feel guilty. What was his problem?

"Come on, pick up your book. We've got a lot to get through today."

His temper wasn't any too sweet, she decided, standing to follow him. Apparently his dinner date last night hadn't done anything much for him.

"Right." He threw himself into his leather chair and faced her. Barely giving her time to open her notebook, he started dictating. Her pencil flew along the page. Her shorthand speed had more than doubled since she'd started working for him.

The opening of the door interrupted them.

"Hello, darling." Shereen St. Clair glided in, wearing a peach-colored slack suit that should have clashed with her red hair but somehow didn't. Bryce stood, and Shereen went straight up to him and kissed him on the mouth.

Caroline felt sure he would push the model to one side because of her own presence in the office. He didn't. Instead he deepened the kiss to a long, passionate one as Caroline sat rooted to her chair. Shocked beyond belief, she watched his hands move to Shereen's hip so he could mould her body closer.

Shereen obviously felt no shame, either, twining her fingers into the dark hair at his nape in a brazen display of ownership. Caroline bit her lip to stop the jealous scream rising up in her throat. On legs that felt so weak she didn't know how they supported her weight, she somehow made it to the door.

"Close the door on the way out." Bryce raised his head. "I don't want to be interrupted on any account." She almost could have sworn he was deliberately trying to get her flustered.

Shereen, giggling like a schoolgirl, locked her arms around his neck and kissed him again.

Caroline, her notebook clutched in a trembling hand, staggered to her typewriter. She started frantically transcribing her notes—anything to keep herself from falling into a screaming heap on the floor. She had finished several letters before Bryce called her back into his office.

Shereen must have departed by another door, the one which led from Bryce's office into the corridor, although that particular door was rarely used. Had he made love to Shereen? Her heart flipped over and her stomach muscles knotted until she felt almost physically ill.

"Ready?" There was just the faintest suggestion of a smile hovering on his lips.

She nodded, beyond speaking. She opened her book and he started dictating again. Pausing for a moment, he lit a cigarette and lounged back in his chair, letting the smoke drift from his nostrils.

"Did we shock you, little Miss Prim?" he asked, giving a naughty schoolboy grin.

Her eyes flew open. What was he playing at now?

"Come on, Caroline. You were shocked, weren't you?"

"I don't know what you mean," she stammered.

"I think you do." He burst out laughing. "I have a luncheon date, so I won't be back until two o'clock."

"Yes, Mr. Harrington. Is that all?"

"Yes. Aren't you interested in knowing who my lunch date is?" he asked with a mocking grin.

"Not particularly." With a superhuman effort she forced her voice to sound careless. She should be nominated for an Oscar. Outwardly calm, inwardly seething, she dared not let her turmoil show.

His eyes darkened, his lips compressed, and she realized her indifference annoyed him. Good. She was a better actor than she thought.

When she had finished typing up all the letters, she put them in Bryce's inbox. He had taken himself off to his luncheon date, giving her a little more time to get her emotions under control.

She left the office at lunchtime, too, not for a romantic tête-à-tête at some intimate little restaurant but to buy a suitable dress, because Andy was taking her out to dinner. He was due home tomorrow morning, on leave from the army officers' academy. He was in his final year and in a few weeks would graduate as a captain. Would he be sent to Vietnam? *Please, God, don't let him be sent over there. It wouldn't be fair.* The family had already sacrificed enough. Two generations of Dennison men had been used as cannon fodder in the world wars. She and Andy were the only members of their family left now.

She caught a bus that ran into the city center. Some of the arcades running off the main streets would have what she wanted. The restaurant she and Andy were going to was an exclusive one. She knew this because she had rung on several occasions to book a table for Bryce. For her birthday on Wednesday, Andy wanted to take her somewhere special this weekend instead of buying a present.

He was two years older than she was, but no brother and sister could have been closer, even though their jealous mother had tried to drive a wedge between them. He was her only living relative now. Their father had been killed in the last days of the Second World War, and their mother had died about three years ago. While she lived, things were relatively easy for them financially, as the government provided her with a war widow's pension and allowances for their education. On her death, the government money stopped, and by the time the estate had been settled there was nothing left.

Andy had volunteered to throw in his studies, but Caroline couldn't let him do that. His heart was set on following in their father's footsteps and becoming an army officer. After much arguing, she had finally persuaded him to stay in school until he got his commission.

Many of his army mates received allowances from their families as well as their government payment. He didn't, but somehow he managed to survive on his army pay. She smiled when she remembered him saying, "I don't take girls out, so that saves me heaps."

After flicking through several racks of dresses she found what she wanted—an ice-blue, pleated dress, the pure silk yolk embossed with gold, frightfully expensive. She justified the extravagance because she wanted Andy to be proud of her, and she didn't need to spend money on accessories because she had shoes and a bag at home that would match. With her dress box in her hand, she hurried outside to catch a bus back to her office.

By the time she arrived, she was breathless. The phone rang and she dashed for it. "Mr. Harrington's secretary. May I help you?"

"Good afternoon, Alexander Harrington here. Put me through to my son, please?"

"I'm sorry, Mr. Harrington, but he won't be back from lunch until about two. May I take a message, or ask him to ring back?"

"Yes, my dear, get him to call me as soon as he comes back, er, it's Miss Dennison, isn't it?"

"Yes, I'm Caroline Dennison."

"I thought so. My wife liked the black opal you helped my son choose."

She almost said, *Your son didn't help, I went shopping on my own*, but restrained herself. "I'm glad. I thought it was beautiful." So it ought to be, considering the price. Sinful, spending so much money on a piece of jewelry. "Is there anything I can help you with, Mr. Harrington?"

"No thank you, this is a family matter. Get him to call me the moment he arrives back. Goodbye." The phone went dead.

Harrington Senior seemed a nice man, never anything but polite. A pity his son didn't take after him. She went to the kitchen, made a cup of coffee and took it back to her office.

She made several telephones calls, chasing up a consignment of missing timber they needed for a new housing estate. How several loads of timber could get lost was a mystery. Theft would be the most likely cause, she thought.

At three o'clock Bryce strolled into her office. Why he always came through here instead of using his own private entrance she could never fathom. Wanted to catch her slacking on the job, maybe?

"Any calls for me?"

"Yes, your father rang. He wants you to call him straight away. Other than that, there wasn't anything I couldn't handle."

He scowled. "What on earth does he want? Couldn't you help him?"

"I offered to, but he said it was a family matter."

"All right, thanks."

"I've finished your typing. Is there anything else you'd like me to do?"

"I have to give a speech at a business dinner on Monday night. I'd like you to type it up for me."

He went to his office and returned with a sheaf of papers. "Do it in double spacing, will you? A rough draft will be fine, thanks." He turned on his heel and went back to his office.

Caroline glanced at the notes. He always used black ink and wrote atrociously. How on earth would she be able to decipher any of it?

She started typing on a plain piece of foolscap paper, stopping every now and again to study what he'd written. On the second page of the speech she came across an alteration with several extra words squeezed in. No matter how hard she tried, even using a magnifying glass, she couldn't decipher it. Nothing else for it but to go and ask him to clarify.

She crossed the carpeted floor of her office and knocked on his door.

"Come in." As she pushed open the door and walked in, she heard Bryce snarl. "I'm not taking her to the dinner. I don't give a damn whose daughter she is. I already have a date."

He stopped speaking, but scowled. The person on the other end of the phone didn't seem to be saying what he wanted to hear.

"I'm telling you, I've already asked someone to accompany me," he ground the words out. "And no, she's not some empty-headed actress." He looked to be getting angrier by the second. Caroline watched him grip the phone. He was trying to keep his temper in check but failing miserably.

"Who?" He shot her a ferocious look. "Caroline," he snapped. "Yes, my secretary. I might need her to take some notes. I'm busy. I'll see you Monday night." He slammed the phone down.

"My father," he explained. "If you're doing anything on Monday night, cancel it. You're accompanying me to a business dinner."

"I am?"

"That's what I said, isn't it? I'd rather put up with you than some bimbo my mother has lined up for me."

"I could have another engagement on Monday night." She wouldn't have cared if royalty were visiting. She'd have put them off to go out with Bryce, but pride stopped her from saying so.

"You'll have to cancel it. I'll call for you about seven. Have you got something suitable to wear? You'll need an after-five frock."

Before Caroline could frame an answer, he went on. "Give me the sundry accounts checkbook. I'll write you out a check so you can go buy yourself something decent."

"You don't have to pay for my clothes." How humiliating. Did he think she was trailer-park trash who didn't know how to dress properly?

"*I'm* not buying your clothes." He gave a nonchalant shrug. "The firm is. We'll claim it as a tax deduction."

Dumbstruck, she meekly handed over the checkbook and he wrote out a check. She couldn't believe her eyes. Surely he couldn't mean it—five hundred dollars?

"It's too much. I don't need to pay that much for a dress." She felt so embarrassed her face was probably as red as a beetroot.

Momentarily his eyes registered surprise, then his lips compressed. "If I'm escorting you anywhere, you'll need at least that much. I won't be seen with a woman who isn't elegant." His voice had an edge to it. "What did you come in to see me for? Not my scintillating company, I'm sure."

"Oh." She had forgotten about his speech. "I couldn't decipher your writing."

"Nothing wrong with my writing."

Who was he trying to kid? She pointed out the words she couldn't understand.

"Let's see." His sudden grin chased away the somber shadows marring his handsome face. "I can't read it myself. Oh, well." He gave a careless shrug. "We'll change it." He proceeded to do so. "There, when you've finished typing that out, you can leave early and shop around for a dress."

"Mr. Harrington, I don't need the money. I bought an after-five frock at lunchtime because I'm going out to dinner at Marianne's tomorrow. I'm sure it would be suitable for Monday's dinner."

"Well, well, fancy that. A woman who isn't trying to squeeze as much money as she can out of a man."

"I'm not like the women you normally mix with. Not every female is trying to see how much she can gouge."

He gave a cynical laugh. "All the women I know check a man's bank balance before going out with him. You're a rarity, little Miss Prim, and I still want you to buy a dress. Call it an early Christmas present. You've earned it. I'm the first to admit I'm not an easy man to work for."

"Thank you." Caroline accepted the check and returned to her desk. When she had finished typing out the speech, she took it in to him. "Is there anything else that needs doing?"

"No, thanks. You might as well go now. By the way, what number is your apartment?"

"Three."

"Good. See you around seven on Monday."

At four o'clock she gathered together her dress box and bag. Standing in the elevator, she debated about what type of dress to buy. If she got something sophisticated, he might see her as a woman. She was a fool, thinking he'd notice her. That wouldn't happen, regardless of what she wore. It was pitiful, this yearning she felt for him, this obsession to be more than a mere secretary.

She wanted to be the woman he loved, the mother of his children. When would she stop torturing herself? She couldn't even attract and hold an ordinary man, let alone one as extraordinary as this.

It seemed ridiculous to be buying another dress. She alighted from the bus in the city center and wandered around until she found a small boutique specializing in after-five wear. She approached the saleslady. "Could you help me select an after-five frock? I'm going to an important function with my boss, and I haven't a clue what to wear."

"There's a markdown rack over there," the woman said helpfully. "Anything on it would be suitable."

"Thanks. I've got a check here from my boss." Caroline pulled it out of her bag.

"No problem at all. We'd be happy to accept it."

Browsing through a rack of markdowns, she found an apricot silk jersey dress, fitted at the bust, with shoestring straps that left her shoulders bare and a skirt that fell into soft swirls at knee level. A wispy see-through bolero top completed the outfit.

The price took her breath away. Even though it had been marked down there wasn't much change left from five hundred dollars. Thank goodness she didn't need to buy new shoes or a bag. With the two boxes now clutched in her hand, she made her way back to the bus stop.

On arrival home, she hung the dresses up. Wait until Kerry saw them—she would be green with envy! Every Friday Kerry brought home take-away fish and chips. It was a late shopping night and the department stores stayed open until nine o'clock. Trevor often worked late, so the girls caught up on their housework then instead of spoiling their weekend with it.

Kerry arrived home right on six o'clock, bringing the fish and chips. Caroline rushed to greet her, eager to tell her friend about the dresses.

"Fancy Mr. High-and-Mighty giving you the money for a new dress," Kerry said. "Although it's reasonable, when you think about it. After all, you are on company business, and he wouldn't want you to look shabby. Could reflect poorly on him," she sneered. "He does have an image to live up to, or at least he thinks he does."

"He's picking me up at seven on Monday," Caroline went on happily.

"Yeah, well, don't get too worked up about it. He's only using you. He'll have you taking notes all night."

"I can't decide how to wear my hair on Monday. What do you think?"

Kerry snorted. "What about Saturday night? Look, Caro, Saturday should mean more to you than Monday. Andy doesn't have much money, but he wants to take you somewhere special. Harrington is loaded and he's taking you to some lousy business dinner, one he's not even paying for."

"Sorry. I'm acting like an idiot. I seem to lose control of my faculties whenever I think of Bryce. It's pathetic." She held her head in her hands. "I only wish I could stop loving him."

Chapter 4

"Hi, girls!" Andy greeted Caroline and Kerry with his usual enthusiasm when he arrived at their apartment on Saturday morning. "I have to be back at camp by Sunday night."

"You can sleep on the couch here. It's quite comfortable," Caroline said.

"Thanks. One of my mates dropped me off about ten miles from here, so I hitched the rest of the way," he explained with a grin.

He was very fair, with corn-colored hair and deep blue eyes. Their mother used to gush about his prettiness, when he was a child. Nothing feminine about him now, Caroline decided, after surviving a rib-cracking hug.

He had matured over the last twelve months. There was a determined jut to his chin, and his youthfulness was changing as the army moulded him into a man. Her heart filled with pride. But what if the army sent him to the jungles of Vietnam? His potential might never be fully achieved. Icy fingers of dread played up and down her spine.

"What's for lunch?" He flung himself down in a chair. "I'm starving."

"Spaghetti on toast." Kerry grabbed a can out of the cupboard and waved it around.

"Sounds good to me."

Caroline had once hoped Andy and Kerry might become an item, even with Kerry's antiwar views, but he treated her in a casual, big-brother fashion, and she reacted like a fond sister. It disappointed Caroline that there were no sparks between them whatsoever.

They ate their spaghetti, washed down with cups of coffee.

Trevor arrived at about one-thirty to take them for a drive. He hadn't met Andy before, but after an initial period of awkwardness between army officer and pacifist, they got on well.

"Where to?" Trevor asked.

"What about Elwood Beach, even if it isn't hot enough to swim," Kerry suggested. Trevor wore casual jeans and a T-shirt, Kerry and Caroline jeans and lacy tops. Glancing at Andy in his faded jeans and too-tight T-shirt, Caroline knew no one would pick him out as an army officer. Safer that way. Violent elements had infiltrated the ranks of genuine antiwar protesters.

After a short drive, they arrived at the beach and spread their rug on the white sand. The girls rolled up the legs of their jeans to let the sun warm their bare legs.

"We should have worn hats," Trevor said. "It's hotter than I thought." He pulled a packet of cigarettes from his jeans pocket and offered them to Andy.

"No thanks, mate. I don't smoke."

"Looks like I'll have to enjoy a coffin nail on my lonesome." Trevor lit his cigarette and smoked it with enjoyment.

Elwood Beach was only a short drive from Melbourne. It was popular and crowded, even on a day like this. A few children paddled in the water, although most of them were building castles or digging in the warm sand.

"Let's go for a walk," Trevor suggested.

As Caroline walked along the water's edge with the others, the waves lapped over her feet. Seagulls flew around them, squawking loudly. Some of these birds were tame, having been fed scraps of bread by beachgoers.

"Sorry, mate, I haven't got anything for you to eat," Andy said to one venturesome bird that hopped near his foot. Finding that this human was a lost cause, the bird soon flew away.

On the way back to where they had left the rug, Kerry and Trevor held hands and whispered together.

"How have you been?" Andy asked Caroline.

"Fine."

"You seem different, sort of sad or something. You wouldn't be keeping anything from me, would you? I mean, if you were in trouble you'd tell your big brother, right?"

"I'm okay, honestly. Except, I've got a crush on

someone who doesn't know I exist." She gave a rueful smile.

"Is that all?" He laughed with relief. "But I mean it. You have changed. It's subtle, but there is something just the same."

"Do you think they might send you to Vietnam after you graduate?" she asked, trying to keep the worry out of her voice.

"I don't know, but I hope so." He thrust his hands in his pockets. "They're conscripting thousands to increase the size of the army, so they'll need officers to lead them. I'd prefer to fight with volunteers, though."

"You don't agree with conscription?" Caroline asked in surprise.

"No. None of the men I'm with like it. We don't think it's right, conscripting men to fight overseas against their will. Drawing their birthdates out of a barrel is criminal." His eyes burned fiercely. "It could turn into a death lottery. I wouldn't want to have that kind of blood on my hands."

Caroline was glad when they caught up with the other two and the discussion ended. The whole Vietnam War issue worried her as she battled with her conscience. If it weren't for Andy being in the army, if it weren't for not wanting to appear disloyal to him, she would probably have joined the antiwar protesters.

They lounged around until it started to get cold. Trevor dropped them off at the apartment. "I'll be back about six to pick you up."

Andy was showered and dressed in his uniform, sitting at the table reading the evening papers, when the girls finished getting ready. He whistled his approval on seeing them.

"Wow, Trev and I will have to fight off every male under forty," he teased.

Caroline felt pleased with her appearance. The dress certainly flattered her figure as it clung in all the right places, and the pale blue material seemed to emphasize the color of her eyes. She had applied a light liquid makeup, some blue eye shadow and a pink pearl lipstick. Her hair, newly washed and dried, fell in a soft cape about her shoulders.

Kerry strutted up and down in her cream georgette tunic with metallic gold trim, pretending to be a model on the catwalk. "Aren't you the handsome soldier boy," she said to Andy, giving him a mock salute, and he grinned.

Trevor arrived a short time later, looking smart in a brown suit and tie with a beige self-striped shirt. "Wow, you girls look terrific." He turned to Andy with a grin. "Do I have to call you 'sir'?"

"No, mate. I'll let you off this time."

****

They arrived at Marianne's restaurant, where without any fuss or fanfare a dinner-suited waiter escorted them to their table. All the tables were set around a circular dance floor. A pink piano reposed on a stage up at the front.

A wine waiter brought them the wine list. Trevor, who professed himself a connoisseur, ordered a bottle of sparkling white wine for the girls and two bottles of crown lager for himself and Andy.

Caroline looked around at the impressive décor. Hurricane lamps hung from the ceiling, casting a subdued glow on the rectory-style tables. She could see that the patrons were a mixture of well-heeled young and middle-aged couples.

As an appetizer, they ordered Avocado Stuffed with Macadamia Nuts on Watercress Puree, which was really half an avocado wrapped in a thin, almost transparent veil of filo pastry. It tasted delicious.

As they ate, the band played softly, never intrusively. It wasn't that type of establishment. The lights were dimmed, the atmosphere romantic.

"How about a dance?" Andy asked.

"Thanks. I didn't know you could dance," Caroline said.

"The army's taught me a few useful pursuits." He chuckled. "Including how to trip the light fantastic. Our kind of music has a lot more beat to it than this morbid stuff, though."

Trevor and Kerry got up, too, and the four of them made their way to the dance floor. Caroline felt proud on seeing the admiring glances her brother received. He looked so handsome in his uniform.

"A lovely young couple," she overheard a middle-aged gentleman remark to his wife. She suppressed a grin because people assumed he was her boyfriend.

"What's so funny?" he asked.

Caroline laughed. "Everyone thinks you're my boyfriend. I can just see their minds ticking over. Isn't she a lucky girl to have such a dashing young officer dancing with her."

"Yeah, well, in some parts of Melbourne they'd be throwing buckets of red paint over me and calling me a murderer."

"I know." Caroline shuddered. "It's awful."

"It doesn't bother me overmuch. Some of those protesters are absolute raving rat bags. Others are genuine people exercising their democratic right."

A few minutes after they returned to their table, the main course arrived. Chicken Maryland, with banana and pineapple, cooked in a crumbed batter. Trevor waited until they finished eating before asking Caroline to dance. Although he was quite an accomplished dancer, he wasn't as light on his feet or as supple as Andy. When the dance finished, their dessert had just been served, her favorite, Strawberry Romanoff.

Later, as she danced again with Andy, a sexy male voice drawled in her ear, "Well, if it isn't Miss Dennison."

She almost collapsed in a heap. Bryce and Shereen were dancing right next to them.

"Oh, hello, Mr. Harrington, Miss St. Clair."

"How are you, darling?" Shereen, superb in a skintight black dress, smiled at Caroline. "My, you are a handsome one," she cooed in Andy's ear.

"Thanks." He grinned. "Caroline thinks I'm handsome, too." The music stopped and Caroline tugged at Andy's hand.

"Would you care to join us for a drink?" Bryce asked, giving one of his devastating smiles.

"No, thanks, we're dining with friends," Andy replied, much to Caroline's relief, as she had been rendered speechless. Fancy meeting Bryce here. Was it pure coincidence, or had he chosen Marianne's knowing she would be here? *Stop it, you fool.* This was one of his favorite haunts, for goodness' sake.

He looked movie-star handsome in a dark navy dinner suit with matching tie and pale blue silk shirt. A red silk handkerchief poked out of his breast pocket.

"We're celebrating Caro's birthday," Andy said, by way of explanation.

"I didn't know it was your birthday, Caroline."

She liked the way Bryce drawled her name. "It's actually on Wednesday," Caroline said.

"But I could only get leave this weekend," Andy explained.

Bryce's speculative gaze drifted over her and she flushed at his scrutiny. Did he like what he saw?

"Which table are you at?" he asked.

"The one over there." She waved an arm vaguely.

"Table ten," Andy filled in.

The music started up again. "We'll change partners," Bryce shocked her by saying. The next minute she was in his arms and waltzing around the dance floor. It was magic being held by him. Oh, God, how many times had she dreamed of this? She glanced at Andy, who appeared quite happy to be dancing with the glamorous redhead.

"You dance well," Bryce whispered in her ear, his warm breath fanning her cheek.

If only the music would last forever. He was a superb dancer, holding her firmly, close but not too close. He could glue her to his side and she wouldn't complain. How pathetic could a girl get?

She inhaled the subtle scent of his tangy citrus aftershave lotion, a change from the Old Spice worn by most of the men she knew.

She felt his heartbeat, strong and steady, but her own heart raced and she prayed he didn't notice. She would die of humiliation if he ever found out the extent of her feelings for him. He would probably fire her, to avoid embarrassment.

She melted against him, her cheek resting against the soft fabric of his jacket until she realized what she was doing.

"Sorry." She made to pull away.

"No." His hand in the small of her back kept her close.

She felt his hard thighs brushing against her own

through the thin fabric of her dress. Agony and ecstasy in equal measure.

"You look lovely tonight." His soft compliment stirred the loosened strands of her hair.

All too soon the music stopped. It must have been a short bracket. She felt as if they had been dancing for only a couple of seconds. If the bracket had lasted two hours it still wouldn't have been long enough.

He escorted her back to her table with a firm but now impersonal hand under one elbow. The episode on the dance floor might never have happened.

Kerry and Trevor hadn't returned to the table yet, but Shereen had almost draped herself over Andy.

"Enjoy your evening," Bryce said. Taking Shereen by the arm, he walked towards the other side of the room.

"Is he the one you like?" Andy asked, as he held a chair out for her.

Was she that transparent? "Yes, he's my boss."

"I didn't think much of him. Too arrogant and sure of himself. Didn't go for the skinny chick with him, either. She kept pumping me for information, but I didn't tell her anything. Asked if we were going steady."

"What did you say?" Caroline knew everything would be relayed to Bryce.

"I just sort of laughed and didn't really say anything. Not hard. She's decorative but dumb."

Kerry and Trevor's return interrupted their conversation.

"Let's call the waiter over and order a bottle of bubbly," Andy decided. Hardly had he spoken the words when the wine waiter appeared like a magic genie with a bottle of champagne resting in a silver bucket.

"Compliments of Mr. Harrington," he said.

"Thanks." Andy grinned. "Saves us buying it."

Trevor, glancing at the label as the waiter filled their glasses, whistled. "Dom Perignon. Must have cost a packet."

"I met my boss on the dance floor."

"You mean Mr. High-and-Mighty is here?" Kerry remarked, sipping the champagne with enjoyment. "And he sent this over? Wonder what he wants?"

"It's Caro's birthday," Andy put in. "Don't you like

him?"

"No."

"I didn't think much of him, either. Too arrogant and self-assured, I thought."

"Typical bloody establishment," Trevor sneered.

"Yeah, he's so far up himself."

"Kerry!"

"Oh, all right, Caro." Kerry threw her hands in the air in mock surrender. "Because it's your birthday, I won't say another word about him."

They drank the champagne, danced a few more times without seeing Bryce again, and left.

When the car stopped at the apartment, Andy jumped out straight away, pulling Caroline after him.

"We'll leave you two lovebirds alone for a while." He laughed. "Don't fall over me on the way in. Remember, I'm sleeping on the couch."

They said their goodnights, and Caroline and Andy went into the apartment.

"I'll make up your bed now," she said as soon as she put her purse down.

"Don't worry, just a pillow and a blanket will be all right." He started undoing the buttons on his uniform jacket.

"You're not stripping off out here, I hope."

"Nah." He gave a grin. "I'll get changed in the bathroom. I've even brought some pajama pants so I'll be respectable, little sister."

"Thanks for taking me out tonight. I enjoyed it."

He leaned over and kissed her cheek. "Happy birthday for Wednesday. I wish I could afford to buy you a present, as well, but I'll have a bit of money saved up by Christmas, so I'll buy you something special then."

"Thanks. But you don't have to." She gave him a hug. "I'll just use the bathroom to clean off my makeup. Kerry won't be in for a while. Did you like Trevor?"

"I did. Surprising, when he's so anti-establishment. He reckons he's going to burn his call-up papers."

"He can't. He'll get into trouble."

"I know. I told him the government is going to clamp down hard. They've already jailed a couple of conscientious objectors. Get Kerry to try and talk him out of it, okay?"

The next morning, Caroline was awakened by Andy bringing them toast and tea in bed. "See, I'm paying for my board and lodging."

He was freshly showered, his damp hair still managing to form tight curls even though he wore it cut short.

"Gosh," Kerry groaned. "How can you be so cheerful? It's indecent. I feel half dead."

"Well, if you stay up half the night pashing on, serves you right."

"Andy!" Caroline admonished her brother. "You're not in camp now. I'm half dead, too, and I didn't stay up necking. It must have been the champagne."

"You've got a hangover, sister dear, that's your trouble. Can't hold your liquor." Laughing, he walked out of the bedroom.

"This is a lifesaver. I'm really fuzzy-headed." Caroline raised herself carefully. "That Dom Perignon packs a punch."

Kerry winced as she sat up. "I reckon we both have got hangovers."

After Caroline had showered and dressed in jeans and a T-shirt, she went out to talk to her brother. He had not only cooked their breakfast but cleaned up the kitchen afterward, as well.

"You're quite domesticated." She smiled as she sat at the table with a second cup of tea.

"I'm full of surprises, aren't I? I'll be pushing off soon. If I make it out to Caulfield, I can get a lift back with another mate, but he's leaving before lunch. Try to get Kerry to make Trevor see reason, will you? He's not a bad bloke. I wouldn't like to see him get into trouble."

After Andy left, Kerry went out with Trevor, but Caroline stayed home. She didn't know whether or not Kerry believed her story of wanting a lazy afternoon on her own. The real reason was that she wanted to go over the happenings of last night, especially the wonderful part of the evening spent in Bryce's arms.

Chapter 5

On Monday morning Caroline arrived at work early and set about tidying up the filing cabinet.

"Good morning, Caroline."

When her boss spoke from behind her, she nearly dropped the bundle of files in her arms.

"Good morning, Mr. Harrington."

His tailored brown suit fitted him like a glove, and she liked his fancy brown-and-black patterned tie. Although his suits and shirts were always conservative, he favored multi-colored silk ties. He looked so handsome her heartbeats escalated. She forced herself not to stare at him. Ogle was probably the right word, or maybe drool.

"Thanks for the champagne on Saturday."

"That's all right." A faint smiled turned up the corners of his mouth. "I hope you and your friends enjoyed it."

"Oh, we did, but we all had headaches next morning." She smiled at him, but when he scrutinized her face, let her eyelashes flutter down in case he read the yearning in her eyes.

"I have to go out to a building site. You'd better come with me."

"Yes, Mr. Harrington. Now?"

"Yes, please."

She picked up her notebook and pencils and put them in her bag. Glancing at her stiletto heels, she grimaced slightly.

"Not particularly suitable, are they? You'll have to be careful where you walk. Can't have you breaking your ankle. I don't know of anyone else who'd put up with me like you do." He laughed. "And before you raise your hackles, I meant it as a compliment."

She followed him out of the office. He allowed her to precede him into the elevator. Remembering the last time they'd shared an elevator together, she hoped it would jerk and throw her against him again. Any contact with him, no matter how brief, would be bliss. Better still if it stopped mid-floor for a couple of hours. Unfortunately, the ride was as smooth as glass. She could have screamed in disappointment.

On the ground floor he held the door open for her and they crossed the foyer together.

"I adore your car," she told him, snuggling into the soft, luxurious seat of the Jaguar.

"It's not bad."

As they drove through the inner suburbs of Melbourne she chanced a glance at him every now and again. He didn't speak and neither did she, although it wasn't an unpleasant silence.

They headed towards the outer bayside suburbs and after half an hour or so pulled up at the construction site. Caroline knew Harrington Constructions was in the process of constructing a large retirement village here. Plans included an assembly hall, an indoor swimming pool and landscaped gardens. The units would be self-contained, each having two bedrooms as well as its own lockup garage. For old people unable to continue living in their own homes, it would be a perfect setup. That's if you were wealthy enough to pay for it.

A caretaker would be living in the village, as well as a full-time nursing sister. Bryce thought of everything. It would be another successful venture for the company.

Bryce parked the car, and they walked to meet the foreman, who was waiting near his office. Caroline could see that the workers were in the process of constructing a road.

A young man driving a bulldozer called out. "How are you going, gorgeous?"

"Damn it all," Bryce snapped at the man approaching them on foot. "Can't you control these men of yours?"

"Nothing I can do about it, Mr. Harrington. They're just showing their appreciation of a pretty girl." The foreman winked at Caroline behind Bryce's back, and she stifled a giggle.

"Come on, boss, I'll show you the plans, so you can see how far we've got." He rolled out some papers and Bryce followed his finger as the man pointed out how they were progressing.

"I thought we'd be much farther advanced than this," Bryce said, an edge to his voice.

"Yeah, well, there's been trouble with the unions. A transport strike held us up quite a bit. After that, the concrete suppliers went on strike, and that put us behind some more."

The foreman didn't appear to be too worried about the delay, but one glance at Bryce's face told Caroline he wasn't happy with the holdups.

"Can't you hurry things along? I want this finished before summer ends."

"We're doing the best we can, boss. The men have been working heaps of overtime. With the Christmas break coming up, I don't think we've got a hope in hell of completing it in the time frame you set."

"I realize that, now. Couldn't you persuade the men not to take their holidays until the job's finished? I'd be prepared to pay a bonus to any man willing to work."

"Have a heart, Mr. Harrington. Most of these men have got school-aged kids. They like to go away with their families over the long school break."

"Don't you think I know that?" Bryce gave an exasperated sigh. "See what you can do. They could have an extra week or so later on in the year, plus a bonus. Put it to them, will you, Duncan?"

"All right, but I don't hold out much hope. Most of them will have planned their holidays by now."

"Do what you can. Even if half a dozen men stay on the job, it will help. Not much point in my hanging around here now. Come on, Caroline. I'll call in again next week."

She followed Bryce back to the car, with the foreman just a step or two behind them. He opened the passenger door for her.

"Thanks."

She could tell by the way Bryce's hands clutched the steering wheel that he was angry.

"What a waste of damn time," he bit out, lighting a cigarette before starting the engine.

By the time they arrived back at the office, it was right on lunchtime. She went straight to her desk and put her bag in the drawer while Bryce stalked into his office.

"Oh, darling, there you are." Caroline heard Shereen's saccharine sweet greeting before the door closed with a click. Why did she cling to the hope that Bryce might feel something special for her one day? She had more chance of finding the pot of gold at the end of the rainbow.

Why didn't he take Shereen to the business dinner tonight? She looked decorative enough. Maybe he did need someone to take shorthand notes, after all. She typed a letter out, through a blur of tears. Would she never learn? To Bryce Harrington she was merely a capable pair of hands that ensured his office ran on oiled wheels. Nothing more, nothing less.

About twenty minutes later, Bryce and Shereen strolled out of the office together. "I'm going to lunch, should be back about two," he threw over one shoulder. Shereen waved to Caroline, who could hear the woman's twittering laugh as they disappeared down the corridor.

He didn't come back until nearly three o'clock. *Some lunch.* She was tempted to tell him she didn't want to go to the dinner after all. She didn't say it, of course. A few crumbs were better than nothing, and there was the dress the company had paid for. On principle she had to wear it.

She arrived home about five-thirty and had a quick cup of tea. Kerry had already left with Trevor to attend a silent vigil organized by the "Save our Sons" organization. They didn't have the luxury of a bath, so she took a long, leisurely shower. After washing her hair, she dried it with her drying wand, lifting up the strands and letting them drop until they fell in silky folds about her shoulders.

The burnt orange dress highlighted her pale skin and she felt quite sophisticated. The small cameo locket she wore was a Dennison family heirloom. Because it was a warm evening, she decided against taking a wrap to cover her shoulders.

She had sprayed a pair of high-heeled white sandals to match the frock and knew she had never looked this good before. Marvelous, what an expensive outfit could do for a woman, even a plain Jane like her.

At three minutes past seven, she heard a knock at the door and almost ran to open it. "Count to thirty," she whispered, not wanting to appear too anxious. When she got to twenty-nine, she opened the door.

"Well, Caroline." Bryce smiled, showing a dimple in his chin. "Turn around. You look beautiful." He stared at her as if he couldn't believe his eyes.

"Would you care to come in?" She stepped back a pace as he followed her inside. His eyes took the room in with a single glance, and she didn't need to be a mind reader to know it didn't impress him.

"I'm ready. I just have to collect my bag."

She came back and found him sitting on the couch, one immaculately-clad leg crossed over the other. He rose to his feet the moment she entered the room. In a dark navy dinner suit with velvet lapels, he looked like a Hollywood playboy.

"Aren't you taking an evening jacket or something for your shoulders?" he asked.

"What?" She dragged her gaze away from him. "No, I won't need one; it's still quite warm." Not for a king's ransom would she tell him she didn't have anything suitable.

"Then if you're ready, we might as well go."

"I've got my shorthand notebook in my bag," she told him as they headed towards the door.

"Good. I don't think you'll need to take any notes, but you never know."

He put his hand under her elbow as they walked towards the car. How warm and strong his fingers felt. When he had made sure she was comfortably seated, he strode around to the driver's side and climbed in. Caroline felt like royalty. As they stopped at a set of traffic lights, she couldn't help noticing the envious looks cast her way. Now she knew what Cinderella felt like, going to the ball in a fancy coach. She only hoped she didn't turn into a pumpkin at midnight.

She wasn't a vain girl—quite the reverse, in fact, having been put down most of her life by her mother's disparaging observations. But tonight she looked well, and she sensed Bryce's approval. He didn't speak as they drove along. She didn't know where they were going and didn't like to ask. As it turned out, the dinner was being held in a private convention room at the Hilton Hotel.

Bryce parked the car in the hotel car park; once

again he put his hand under her elbow when she alighted. They received several interested, speculative glances as they made their way up the carpeted stairs leading from the hotel foyer. They stopped at a door embossed with the word "Private" in gold lettering.

They were the last couple to arrive. On Bryce's entry, several middle-aged executives hastened towards him, bringing their partners with them. Bryce introduced her simply as Caroline. He didn't bother giving her surname or to add that she was his secretary.

All the women wore designer clothes, but she knew her dress would pass the closest scrutiny. A drink waiter came past and Bryce asked for two sherries, a sweet and a dry. He gave her the sweet one, keeping the other for himself. She only spoke when addressed directly, but found it easy enough to converse with these women, who thought she must be one of their own kind—wealthy and socially well-connected.

A tall, impeccably-groomed older man came over to them. He had steel gray hair and the same eyes as Bryce, and she knew without doubt it couldn't be anyone but Alexander Harrington.

"Oh, Bryce, there you are."

"Hello, Dad. Didn't mother come?"

"No. You know why, too. She's at home with Ashley and Sybil Fontain."

Bryce gave a careless shrug. "This is Caroline. Caroline, my father."

"Oh, my dear, I do beg your pardon. I didn't realize you were together." He smiled at her and she instantly liked him. She gave a tentative smile back. He surveyed her, taking in every aspect of her appearance without seeming to be rude. Here was a gentleman of the old school. It was written all over him.

"Excuse me, there's someone I want to see for a moment." Bryce strode off, leaving Caroline with his father.

"Well, my dear, would you care for another drink?"

"No, thank you."

He helped himself to a dry sherry and sipped at it thoughtfully. "How long have you been working for the company?"

"About eight months or so." She gave a nervous smile. Alexander made it obvious, without being rude, that he was curious about why Bryce had invited her. She would be interested to know exactly why herself.

Bryce came back. "Sorry about deserting you." He mouthed the polite platitude, but she knew he couldn't care less. She watched him flirting with a striking brunette, who in turn was making cow eyes at him.

"Isn't that Amanda Cleveland, Sir Arthur's daughter?" Alexander asked.

"Yes."

Even Caroline had heard of Sir Arthur Cleveland, the millionaire industrialist. Beauty plus extreme wealth—Amanda just couldn't miss out. Caroline tried to keep her bitter envy under control.

Bryce and Caroline were taken to a table near the front of the stage, while Alexander Harrington was escorted farther down the room. The other people at their table were strangers, although a couple of the men seemed vaguely familiar. Had she seen their pictures in the financial or society pages of the newspapers? Bryce introduced her to them, but none of their names rang any bells, either.

The appetizer consisted of oysters and caviar served in a pastry shell. So this was how the other half lived. She ate slowly, savoring every delicious mouthful.

The men and one of the women seemed quite friendly and Caroline found it easy to strike up a conversation. In fact, she felt so comfortable with one elderly gent, a real honey, they swapped jokes.

Bryce watched Caroline through half-closed, speculative eyes. When animated, her huge eyes shone like blue beacons, her mouth curved into a mischievous smile. She effortlessly had the old geezers eating out of her hand. They were as dull as dishwater, yet she made them laugh.

For the first time, he really surveyed her. On several occasions in the office he'd noticed her slim legs. What man wouldn't? Her pale skin was as smooth as fine porcelain, and he fought the overwhelming urge to touch it. Her well-shaped lips had a vulnerable softness about them when she wasn't smiling. When she leaned forward, he saw her breasts, creamy white and as flawless as the rest of her flesh. What would she taste like? And what the hell was wrong with him?

Relief washed over him when he had to get up and go to the dais to give his speech. Adjusting the microphone to his height, he began confidently and glanced at his notes only now and again. His speech went well, and he nodded his thanks when the clapping died down.

When he returned to the table, Caroline was fulsome with her praise. "That sounded terrific, Mr. Harrington."

"Bryce, please. We aren't in the office now."

"It read well when I typed it out, but when you spoke, the words seemed to come alive."

"Thanks. Glad you approve."

They were served coffee and tiny almond-flavored biscuits, after which everyone started circulating. Bryce clasped Caroline's hand firmly to keep her near him. He wasn't prepared to fathom out why, but he liked having her close. The sweet, subtle perfume of her skin nearly drove him crazy.

"We've got work in the morning, not like some of these people here," he finally whispered.

He still held Caroline's hand as they strolled over to say goodnight to his father.

"Tell Mother I'll be over one evening towards the end of the week."

"All right, son. Goodnight, Caroline. It was a pleasure meeting you."

"Nice meeting you, too, Mr. Harrington," she told him sincerely. "I always wondered what you looked like. Now I know."

"Ah, well, I hope I didn't disappoint you." He chuckled.

"Oh, no. You're just as distinguished as I imagined you would be." She smiled at him as they walked away.

Bryce held her hand as they went out to the car.

"I had a lovely time. Thank you." She smiled at him.

"I enjoyed it, too." Surprisingly he had. Normally he found these functions tedious. He couldn't understand why it had seemed so different tonight. What a damn lie—it was because Caroline was with him.

They drove in silence and Caroline felt her eyes

growing heavy. She woke with a start when the car pulled up outside her place.

"I'm so sorry," she said.

He gave a soft, intimate laugh. "No need to apologize. You didn't snore."

She felt herself blush. Thank goodness he couldn't see it in the darkness. She fumbled with her seat belt. "Thanks once again for a wonderful evening."

She heard his sudden, sharp intake of breathe. How it happened she didn't know or care, but all at once she was in his arms and his mouth was claiming hers in a gentle, exploratory kiss. When her lips responded of their own volition, his kiss deepened. He pulled her closer into his embrace until she half lay across his knees.

He brushed aside one of the straps on her frock and his mouth seared a fiery trail of kisses from ear to throat. His hand cupped her breast and she was shocked when her nipples hardened.

He must have felt her response. "Oh, God," he groaned.

This was absolute madness. "Bryce, please stop." Her body felt as if it had self-combusted. For the first time in her life she felt physical desire. Raw, fiery, hot and desperate. If she didn't stop him right now, she wouldn't be able to summon the willpower to halt his lovemaking. She wanted him to love her, but not like this.

He pulled away at her insistence. "You have hidden fires," he said huskily.

She tidied her clothing while he lit a cigarette, and after inhaling the smoke he regained command of himself once more.

"Come on. I'll see you to your door." They got out of the car and he escorted her to the front door of the apartment, but made no move to touch her again. She inserted the key in the lock. He waited without speaking until she turned the light on.

"Goodnight, Caroline." With a brief wave, he strode off.

She crept inside so as not to waken Kerry. Taking off her dress in the bathroom, Caroline had a quick wash, dragged on her nightgown and crawled into bed.

Having dreamed for months about what Bryce's

kisses would be like, she now knew. Devastating. The passion he so quickly aroused in her was unbelievable, scary. Blood rushed to her head when she remembered how far she'd let him go before calling a halt. Would he think she was the kind of girl who would go all the way on a first date? That she was easy? Fair game because she came from the working class?

Chapter 6

Next morning Caroline groaned when she heard the alarm go off. She felt as if she'd only just fallen asleep. Kerry got up first, which left her to crawl out of bed and fix breakfast. She rinsed her hands, then splashed cold water on her face at the kitchen sink before starting their tea and toast.

"How did it go last night? You were late home." Kerry breezed into the kitchen dressed in her work uniform.

"Terrific, fabulous. He kissed me." Caroline's eyes sparkled. "It was wonderful."

"Don't get too carried away," Kerry warned. "It's quite usual for a man to kiss a woman after he's taken her out, especially if they've both had a couple of drinks. Washes away their inhibitions."

"I can't wait to get to work and see what he says. He might even ask me out again."

Kerry looked ferocious. "My God. You didn't let him go the whole way?"

"What do you mean, the whole way?" *Oh, no.* Caroline felt hot all over. Surely Kerry didn't think...

"You know what I mean. But you didn't, did you, Caro, surely? Just because a man wants to make love to you, it doesn't mean he's in love with you."

"No, he didn't make love to me."

"Thank goodness for that. You should go out with more men. That way you'll get more experience and know what to expect."

"I'll be late," Caroline wailed after glancing at the clock. She bolted down the rest of her breakfast and dashed into the bathroom for a quick shower. She didn't care what Kerry said. Bryce liked her as a woman. She felt certain of it. *He'll probably ask me out again.* She hummed a favorite pop tune as she toweled herself dry.

It was now December, the start of summer, and it was warm. She decided to wear a sleeveless shirt-style frock in a red-and-white-striped cotton, along with red medium-heeled sandals. In case a cool change blew in later, she took a white cardigan as well. She gave her hair a vigorous brush, then applied a touch of lipstick and eye shadow before rejoining Kerry in the kitchen.

As they left the apartment and headed towards the bus stop, Caroline spied the bus at the top of the street. "Come on, Kerry." They sprinted the last few yards and just managed to catch it. Packed as usual, Caroline thought, as she tried to catch her breath.

She glanced at a fellow passenger's newspaper and the headlines screaming *Police arrest dozens of demonstrators*. What had Kerry been up to last night? "How did the protest meeting go?"

"Good. There were about three hundred people at the army barracks. There's a new batch of conscripts being sworn in tomorrow."

"You're fighting a losing battle to win public support. That survey in September found 61% of the population agreed to the war. Don't encourage Trevor to burn his call-up papers. Andy said they've already locked up some conscientious objectors."

"It's immoral, conscripting men to fight in a war thousands of miles away from home. What are you staring at?" Kerry glared at the man standing next to her.

Caroline breathed a sight of relief when she came to her stop. Kerry and Trevor were heading for trouble, and she didn't want to be dragged into it, for Andy's sake. She got off the bus and hurried into the Harrington building.

Once she was in her office, she checked to see if Bryce had arrived. He hadn't, so she inserted some headed paper and started typing out invoices.

Bryce arrived at nine-thirty.

"Good morning." He greeted her in his usual perfunctory manner and headed towards his office.

"Hello, B-, um, Mr. Harrington." Caroline felt as deflated as a punctured balloon. She forced herself to keep on typing by sheer willpower. Thank goodness there was nothing too complicated. Once she had finished the invoices, she took them in for his signature. He didn't raise his head, just kept on writing.

"Put them into the inbox, thanks. I'll sign them

later," he said absently, with the wave of one hand.

He would most likely say something later on, when he wasn't so busy, she decided. He used the phone several times, and her switchboard lit up each time he did. Lunchtime came, and still he didn't say anything to her, so she went out to the kitchen and made a cup of coffee to go with her sandwiches.

After lunch, Bryce buzzed her and she picked up her book and went into his office. Maybe he would say something now. He didn't, just started dictating several long letters. As the day wore on Caroline realized what a fool she was. He wouldn't say anything. What had been the most emotional episode in her whole life was probably a normal occurrence for him when he took out a pretty, willing girl. In all honesty, she couldn't deny being willing. She was sick with embarrassment just thinking about exactly *how* willing.

The fact that he didn't get annoyed at her stopping his lovemaking from going any further proved he thought the matter trivial. He hadn't given it a second thought. Sunk in a deep pit of self-pity and misery, she nearly toppled off her chair when he spoke.

"I just wanted to let you know I'll be out for the rest of the day. I need to go into the Town Planner's office, so I won't bother coming back." He played with his car keys. "Anything you can't handle, refer to Davies. I told him not to trouble himself about coming up here—you can reach him on the phone. If nothing comes up, you might as well leave early, too." He turned on his heel and strode off.

An hour or so later the phone rang. "Good afternoon, Mr. Harrington's office."

"I'd like to speak to Bryce Harrington." The low feminine voice had a husky, sexy quality to it.

"I'm sorry. Mr. Harrington isn't in at the moment. He won't be back until tomorrow."

"Oh! Amanda Cleveland here. Bryce rang me earlier to ask me out tonight. I wanted to check what time he would be picking me up. Do you know where he went?"

It was as if a dagger had been plunged deep into Caroline's heart. "He intended going to the Town Planner's office." She wondered how she managed to speak without screaming.

"Thanks. I'll try him at home." The phone clicked in her ear.

She felt a fool. An evening which meant so much to her had meant so little to him that he asked another girl out on a date the very next night. The fact that it was Amanda Cleveland, the girl he'd flirted with at the business dinner, made it a hundred times worse.

Eventually the day passed and she was able to go home. Caroline was desperate for a good cry but couldn't afford the luxury. She did some washing to fill in time until Kerry arrived, and then they ate dinner watching the portable television set in the lounge room.

"Did Harrington say anything to you?" Kerry asked the dreaded question.

"No. He didn't say a word." Before she could stop herself, she told Kerry about Amanda.

"You can't compete with a chick like that. Daddy is loaded, he's been knighted and, according to the society pages, she's quite attractive. She'd be an irresistible challenge to a man like Harrington." Kerry put a forkful of food in her mouth and swallowed it in an angry gulp. "I tried to warn you how cruel and arrogant he is. The irony of it all is that you'd be a perfect wife for him. But of course, men can be so stupid, ignoring the obvious."

"Why should Bryce get married?" Caroline went on bitterly. "He gets everything he wants from women without a wedding ring." Cursing herself for being such a blind fool, she blinked away the tears burning at the back of her eyes.

"Why don't you leave, get a job somewhere else? You're only heading for heartbreak, staying on there," Kerry said.

"I know I'm an idiot, but I can't help how I feel. Bryce Harrington is like an incurable disease. I've tried to fight my feelings for him, but I can't." She didn't want to talk about it any more, so she changed the subject. "Did you tell Trevor what Andy said?"

"Yeah, for all the good it did." Giving a resigned shrug, Kerry went out to the kitchen to make them each a cup of hot chocolate. As soon as Caroline finished her drink she retired to bed. She was absolutely exhausted.

When Caroline arrived at work the next day, Bryce

was already in his office. Switching her typewriter on, she started typing a letter she had repeated several times yesterday because she had been so upset after Amanda's call.

"Oh, you're in." Bryce's voice startled her. "About time, too."

No *Good morning, how are you*, she noted. Nothing.

"I'm not late. I don't start until nine and it's just after eight-thirty."

"Don't quibble, girl. I've got some urgent work I want to dictate."

She picked up her notebook and, feeling sad and dispirited, trailed after him. The phone rang. He grabbed it. "What! Don't gabble, man. Strike! For God's sake, get them back on the job. Offer them anything you like. I want that estate finished by Christmas." He banged the receiver down. "Now, where were we? Oh, yes." He took a couple of deep breaths and started dictating.

Caroline didn't know whether she was slow and clumsy or whether he spoke too fast because he was angry, but she kept having to ask him to repeat some of the words.

"What's wrong with you? I've had a gutful of incompetent staff. This is a business I'm trying to run, not a place where you can loaf at my expense."

"I've apologized."

"I don't want your apology. Just do what I pay you for."

"I can't work if you keep yelling at me. It makes me nervous."

He lost his temper at this point and shouted at her. His tongue was a circular saw cutting her into tiny pieces.

When she couldn't stand his ranting a moment longer, she turned to flee in the middle of his tirade. He leapt from his desk and caught hold of her arm.

He spun her around. "Don't walk out on me when I'm speaking."

"What the hell is going on?" Geoff Davies marched into the office.

At the sound of the older man's voice, Bryce dropped his hand and stepped back a pace.

"Are you all right?" the older man asked Caroline, his

eyes full of concern.

"Yes, thanks. Excuse me." She turned and fled. Out in the tearoom she sat on a chair and sobbed.

The pressure of Bryce's fingers on her arm had been slight, but she felt as if her heart had been clawed into slivers. She heard the phone ringing but didn't care. It could ring for all eternity. After several rings it stopped.

How long she remained huddled in the chair with her head in her hands she didn't know. Someone touched her shoulder, and she raised tear-drenched eyes and looked straight into Bryce's face. A muscle convulsed in his jaw, and his tan receded slightly.

"I'm sorry, Caroline. I lost my temper. Don't cry any more. I'll order a cab to take you home."

She stared at him with trembling lips. She couldn't speak. Words were beyond her.

"My God, I didn't mean to upset you. The last twelve hours have been absolute hell, and I took it out on you. Please, don't cry."

He put his arms around her to draw her to her feet, and she buried her face in his chest. His hands ran gently, soothingly over her hair.

"You've got pretty hair, soft, silky," he murmured. "I like the smell of it, too. Don't cry any more." He took her chin in one hand, raised her damp face and started brushing the tears away with his fingertips.

"Oh, Bryce, why are you so mean to me?" she whispered tremulously.

"I don't know. I've always been hot-tempered. I guess as you're the closest person to me, you cop it." He held her firmly. "You're a sweet girl," he whispered. The words washed over her like a gentle breeze, and she wanted to stay in his arms forever, but she couldn't. When she pushed at his chest, he let her go.

"You've got a staunch supporter in Geoff. He just about blew my head off after you left." He gave a rueful smile. "Are you okay now?"

"Yes. I don't need to go home. I'll go to the washroom and tidy myself up."

"Are you sure?" He sounded so concerned she almost started crying again.

"Yes." Her lips quivered into a sad little smile as she

turned away.

After she left the room, Bryce lit a cigarette and drew on it savagely. What the hell was wrong with him, attacking the girl like that? It wasn't her fault that his mother's nagging insistence on him taking a wife and producing the appropriate offspring got him down. God only knew how far he would have gone if Geoff hadn't intervened. He cursed under his breath. If she wasn't so placid, he wouldn't let fly or bully her so often, he was honest enough to admit.

He stalked back to his office, puffing moodily on the cigarette. He threw himself into his chair and brooded. It had been an unmitigated disaster, inviting Amanda Cleveland to his parents' home last night. The only thing he could say in favor of his mother was that she didn't start badgering him until Amanda left the room with his father to view the Harrington art collection.

His mother appeared quite taken with Amanda. He could almost hear her now.

"Think of it, darling. Her father has a knighthood. Such a perfect wife for you."

He was attracted to her, but only in the most carnal way. He couldn't see himself married to anyone just yet, let alone her. She was a selfish, willful creature who suited his purposes—to help him get rid of Shereen.

Why did women have to get possessive after a few dates? He never led any of them to believe he was interested in a long-term relationship or marriage. He clenched his fist on the desk. If it weren't for the fact that he enjoyed the battle to remain at the top of the business world, he would throw everything in and become a recluse somewhere. He gave a wry grin. Living alone wouldn't be a problem, but celibacy might be.

He heard the typewriter start up. Thank God, Caroline had returned. He couldn't help wondering about her. She didn't have much money to spare, her clothes and apartment proved that, yet she always wore an air of quiet dignity. She spoke well, as did the young officer she'd been with the other night. He had private school written all over him.

The Military Academy only took the best candidates, even with the war in Vietnam. He either had to be brainy or have family connections. Probably both. How did Caroline meet him? More importantly, what were her feelings towards him?

He didn't know why, but he hated to think of her becoming involved with the young man. It must be because he didn't want to lose a capable secretary. That was why it concerned him so much. He didn't dare dwell on any alternative.

It was Caroline's birthday tomorrow. He would make amends for losing his temper by giving her a birthday present. Women always reacted well to an expensive bribe. Maybe he could take her out to dinner, as well. After all he'd done to hurt her, it was the least he could do.

He had been debating about asking Amanda to dine with him, but decided against it. She would keep until another time. It was far more important to make amends to Caroline. He would have to control his volatile temper, too. Feeling happier now for having solved his dilemma, he started on some statistical work he'd been deferring for weeks.

****

Caroline worked steadily, now recovered from her weeping episode. The sensible part of her mind castigated her for not resigning on the spot. The romantic side of her nature was prepared to suffer any indignity to be near Bryce. What a weak, pathetic person she had become. She was fast fulfilling her mother's prophesy about never amounting to anything, never being able to attract a man.

When she'd finished the typing, she took it in to Bryce. He glanced up as she entered.

"Put them there, thanks." He bent his head and scrutinized a long line of figures, so she started out of the room.

"Caroline."

"Yes." She swung around.

"Are you okay?"

She nodded.

"Don't go yet, I want to ask you something. Would you have dinner with me tomorrow night?"

"Dinner? With you? I—"

"You've no other engagements?"

She shook her head.

"Good. I'll pick you up at seven. I know of a cozy place we can go to. You don't need to dress up for it, either."

"Sounds nice, thank you."

"You might as well go home now. There's nothing else needs doing here." He inclined his head in dismissal.

Hurrying back to her desk, she tried to keep a lid on her excitement. She told herself not to get too carried away. He was only taking her out to make up for his mean treatment earlier, but she didn't care. The reason didn't matter. He was taking her out. She would gladly go anywhere with him. *You fool, you pitiful fool, falling for such a bribe.*

She tidied up her desk, left the office, and on the bus going home she daydreamed about going out with Bryce. What would she call him? She would love to be able to call him Bryce again, but didn't dare, unless he suggested it. She wouldn't call him Mr. Harrington, either, she decided with a sudden spurt of spirit.

On arrival home, she made a cup of tea before going into a cleaning frenzy. She wanted the apartment to look its best in case he came in, and she wouldn't have much time on Wednesday to clean it up. The fact that it was her birthday made it all the more thrilling.

"You'll never guess what happened." Caroline ambushed her friend the moment she stepped inside. "Bryce is taking me out for dinner tomorrow." She didn't mention about the happenings of the day.

"I hope you know what you're doing." Kerry had never met Bryce, but Caroline knew her friend disliked him. She shouldn't have complained so often about his arrogance and moodiness. Her constant complaints about the way he carried on made things sound worse than they really were.

If she hadn't been in love with him, she wouldn't have given his behavior a second thought. He didn't use foul language or throw things at her like one executive she'd heard about. A girl she'd attended secretarial college with worked for some lecher who kept squeezing her breasts and pinching her on the backside, yet she stayed with him because the job paid well. At least Bryce acted like a gentleman in that respect.

Chapter 7

Wednesday dawned warm and sunny. Caroline worked steadily, trying to keep her excitement in check. Bryce dashed in and out of the office several times, but apart from a brief good morning, he spoke only about business matters.

Mr. Davies, Bryce and his father were members of an eight-man board who held their monthly meetings on Wednesdays. She always took down the minutes.

"How are you, Caroline?" Alexander Harrington greeted her with a cheerful smile. "Did you enjoy the business dinner?"

"Yes, thank you." It wasn't the business dinner she remembered from that evening, but Bryce's fiery kisses.

She ate lunch at her desk, then started typing up the minutes for the last meeting of the year. Just before clock-off time, Bryce poked his head around the door.

"You haven't forgotten our dinner date, have you?"

Forgotten it? She'd thought of nothing else. "No, I haven't forgotten." She smiled at him.

"Good, you can go now. I'll pick you up about seven."

She rushed home, had a shower and washed her hair. By this time Kerry was home, and she not only helped Caroline put her hair up in a topknot, leaving a few wispy strands to form a half fringe, but loaned her a pair of gold prism drop earrings. The pale aqua dress Caroline chose to wear had a double-ruffled lace collar, pintucked bodice and flared skirt, and sported cut-out shoulders with delicate scalloped edges.

"You look terrific," Kerry enthused. She was a supportive friend, even if she didn't like Bryce.

Caroline paced the floor. Suppose he didn't turn up? Right on seven o'clock someone knocked on the door, and she hurried toward it.

Kerry signaled her to take it slowly. "Keep him waiting for a bit," she mouthed. "You don't want to seem overeager."

Caroline counted to twenty before opening the door. Bryce's hand was raised, ready to knock again. He looked devastating in a chocolate brown suit with a cream silk, open-necked shirt. This man was movie star material.

"Come in." Her heart skipped a beat when she saw the appreciative gleam in his eyes. He liked what he saw. Her appearance hadn't let her down. She stepped back a pace so he could enter the apartment.

"Kerry, this is Mr. Harrington."

"Bryce," he put in smoothly. "We're not in the office now. How are you, Kerry?"

"All right."

Caroline was shocked when her friend stayed where she was, with a jean-clad leg hooked over the arm of the couch. It wasn't like Kerry to act so bad-mannered in front of a visitor.

"If you're ready, Caroline, we'll go. Goodnight, Kerry."

"Have a nice time, Caro."

Bryce closed the door behind them with a thud. It didn't take a genius to know he was angry at Kerry's snub. Caroline was disappointed Kerry hadn't even tried to hide her animosity.

They went down the passageway and out into the street to where the Jaguar was parked. *I'll bet the sight of such a prestigious car set a few neighborhood tongues wagging,* she thought with a little thrill.

Ever the gentleman, Bryce helped her into the car with a hand under one elbow. They didn't speak as they drove along. She was too nervous and he seemed preoccupied.

After driving for about fifteen minutes they came to the restaurant, a double-storied terrace house built from bluestone blocks.

"Good evening, Mr. Harrington." The manager met them at the door and ushered them inside. Obviously Bryce was well known. How many other women had he brought here?

They were escorted to a table set for two, in a secluded corner. Once seated, Caroline looked around with interest. Hurricane lamps hung from the ceiling. The lighting was subdued and intimate, discreet ambience surrounding them.

"What a terrific place." She smiled her pleasure, and he squeezed her fingers.

"You look beautiful tonight, not at all like my efficient little secretary." He was only teasing, but the word "my" made her heart sing.

A bottle of vintage champagne arrived, and they drank from crystal flutes.

"Happy birthday, Caroline." They clinked glasses.

Caroline sipped her drink, enjoying every mouthful. It was cool and delicious. "This is the nicest champagne I've ever tasted."

He gave a soft, intimate chuckle, causing her heart to flutter like a caged bird.

They both chose avocados with walnut mayonnaise as an appetizer. When the band struck up a slow, romantic number, he asked her to dance. She floated into his arms when they reached the tiny dance floor, where he held her close and she once again thrilled at the touch of his hard, muscled thighs brushing against hers. Closing her eyes, she rested her cheek against his chest, swaying in time to the music. If this turned out to be a dream, she never wanted to wake up.

His breath stirred her hair, and she smelled the subtle male scent of him, some expensive citrus aftershave and the faintest whiff of tobacco. If only the music would go on forever.

"Have you gone to sleep on me?" He whispered in her ear.

Caroline laughed. "It wouldn't take much to rock me off, the music is so relaxing, and you're nice to lean against."

He chuckled. "I must remember that. So, I'm nice to lean against. You're refreshingly different."

They returned to their table. Before the main course had been served, Bryce pulled a small, neatly wrapped box from his pocket and gave it to her. "Happy birthday."

"Thank you, but I didn't expect a present. I don't remember mentioning my birthday."

"Your army friend told me on Saturday night."

She undid the package to reveal a jeweler's box.

Inside, on a plain gold chain, rested a black opal.

"It's beautiful, but I...I couldn't accept an expensive present like this."

"Why not? I thought you must like black opals, since you chose one for my mother."

"I do. They're exquisite."

"Accept it from me, please. Don't worry about the expense. I can afford it."

Her eyes filled with tears.

"You're crying?"

"Yes," her voice wobbled. "No one has ever given me such a beautiful gift before. I'll treasure it always."

When the tears overflowed and ran down her cheeks, he leaned across the table and wiped them away with his thumb, a gentle action that was almost her undoing. She had to force herself not to grab hold of his hand and rest it against her heart.

The main course, roast duckling cooked with cherries, was accompanied by a salad. It tasted sensational, and she enjoyed every mouthful. What an unforgettable night! She felt as though she were floating on a silver cloud, bound for paradise.

Between courses, they danced. The night flew on golden wings. They finished off with Irish coffee. As they danced the last bracket, Caroline sighed with pleasure.

"This has been the most wonderful night," she breathed.

He pressed her body into his and held her there with a hand on either hip. She could feel his mouth nuzzling the side of her throat. What exquisite pleasure. Deadly dangerous, but exquisite.

"We'll go now. It's nearly closing time," he said huskily and led her back to the table so she could pick up her gold evening bag. He peeled off several twenty-dollar notes and dropped them in the dish for the waiter to collect.

Hand in hand, they left the restaurant. The evening was cool but not cold as they strolled towards the car. The sky sparkled with twinkling stars while the moon sailed the sky like some ghostly galleon on black velvet seas.

"Did you enjoy yourself?" he asked softly, as if he too didn't want to break the magic spell enveloping them.

"Oh yes," she whispered dreamily. "I'll never forget it."

After they drove off, his hand closed over hers, warm and strong. Caroline felt on top of the world. All too soon they arrived back at the apartment. He turned off the motor. She heard a click and the seat slid back, giving them more leg room. He drew her into his arms, and his head blotted out the star-studded night sky as his mouth covered hers.

He tempted and teased her lips until they quivered and opened so she could feel his tongue making a tentative exploration of her mouth. A surge of desire raced through her. His hand cupped her breast for a moment; for the merest fraction of a second his thumb caressed her nipple. When he moved away she felt bereft.

"Would you care to come in for a coffee?"

He hesitated. "I wouldn't like to disturb your friend."

"Kerry's not home, she's gone out with Trevor."

Caroline didn't want the evening to end yet. "Come on, you needn't stay long. It's only eleven o'clock." She was playing with fire and knew it.

"I could do with a coffee," he admitted. "Thanks. I will come in."

He locked the car, then took her hand as they made their way to the apartment foyer. She fumbled with the key, and he took it from her unsteady fingers and unlocked the door. When she turned on the light, they both blinked at the sudden glare. "I think I'll put this off and switch on the TV lamp."

"Good idea." He followed her into the room.

"Sit on the couch," she invited. "It's the most comfortable."

"Thanks." He sat down, stretching his long legs out in front of him, crossing them at the ankle.

"Would you prefer tea or coffee?"

"Coffee, but in a minute. I haven't finished kissing you yet."

He took her hand, pulling her down to sit next to him.

"I've enjoyed tonight, Bryce."

"Good." She felt his fingers moving in her hair. "I like it better loose." He pulled out the pins, causing the soft strands to tumble over her shoulders. "Beautiful," he muttered, burying his face in it. "Smells good, too."

He took her lips with a demanding passion. Nothing gentle about his possession this time. She trembled with emotion as she gave him the response he sought. As his passion intensified, so did hers.

He rained kisses over her face and throat. His tongue, flicking and darting in her mouth, entwined with hers, tasting, but still not fully satisfied.

"Kiss me," he urged huskily.

She did so, exploring his mouth tentatively with her tongue at first but gaining in confidence. His hand caressing her breast through her frock aroused her to unfamiliar desire.

Her trembling fingers unbuttoned his shirt and she buried her face in the soft whorls of hair on his chest. She could feel his heart pounding, smell his male scent, and hear the throbbing, primeval music of sexual desire.

He found the buttons and undid the front of her frock. Pushing it down to her waist, he quickly did the same to her bra. She gasped in delight as his mouth closed over her bare breast and he suckled the rosy nipple into life. She couldn't believe what he was doing to her. How he made her feel. Wanton, truly alive for the first time in her life.

His body half covered hers, his weight pressing her into the couch. He raised his mouth before taking her lips again in a fiery expression of raw need. She didn't feel him pushing away her skirt, only felt his fingers caressing the bare flesh of her thigh. Even with her lack of experience there was no mistaking his intention.

"Oh, Bryce." She sighed with ecstasy as his hand cupped her feminine mound.

He continued touching her, becoming more intimate, his fingers sliding under the leg of her panties so he could stroke her soft feminine curls. Did he feel the sudden warm wetness as need surged through her? It raged white hot, like a wildfire burning out of control.

"You want me, don't you, darling?" his voice sounded thick with desire. "Stop me now, if you don't."

Voices coming from outside the door shattered their fiery passion and instantly doused it.

"Kerry's home," Caroline said in a panic.

"Hell." He rolled away and started buttoning up his shirt.

Trevor and Kerry must have been kissing each other at the door, as silence reigned for a few moments, giving the pair inside time to tidy up their clothing.

"I think I'd better skip the coffee." He stood up. "Good night." He lit a cigarette with trembling hands and started across the room just as the door opened.

"Oops, sorry. Did I interrupt anything?" Kerry didn't sound the least bit sorry.

"I was leaving anyway." Bryce nodded to Trevor, raised his hand in a salute which encompassed them all and left.

"I'm off to bed. Goodnight, Kerry, Trevor." Caroline escaped to the bedroom and got ready for bed. She could still feel the pressure of Bryce's lips on hers. Feel his hands roaming over her heated body. Smell his special male scent and the musky perfume of her own arousal.

Kerry came to bed not long after her, but Caroline pretended to be asleep. Her friend would be bursting with curiosity, but she felt too vulnerable to parry any questions tonight. She just wanted to lie there savoring her magical evening.

****

Next morning at work Bryce greeted her as usual. Last night might never have happened. Halfway through the afternoon, Amanda Cleveland arrived, demanding to see Bryce. Caroline didn't like Shereen over much, probably because of jealousy as much as anything else, but Amanda set her teeth on edge.

This woman was arrogance personified. The way she spoke and held herself, sweeping into the office as if she owned it.

"Bryce will see me," she stated confidently when Caroline tried putting her off by saying he was unavailable. Unavailable forever, if Caroline Dennison had any say in it—au revoir, farewell, good riddance, Amanda.

In the end, Amanda pushed past and minced across the office. She didn't bother knocking, just opened the door and went in. About ten minutes later the buzzer sounded, and Caroline picked up her book and went into Bryce's office.

"Caroline, make Miss Cleveland some coffee, will you, please? I might as well have one, too, while you're at it."

"Black with no sugar," Amanda put in coolly and draped herself across a chair. Her bare legs were well tanned and her dark hair had recently benefited from an expert cut and set. She wore a white linen miniskirt with a matching low-necked top, absolutely plain but so well cut that even on a broomstick it would have looked sensational. The miniskirt exposed most of her thighs. She moved her legs, parting them in brazen invitation.

Caroline hurried out of the room. Jealousy burned her up. She nearly self-combusted. No wonder he forgot about her so quickly. She pushed the plug of the percolator so hard into the electric socket she was surprised it didn't come out the other side of the wall. The china cups and saucers would be in order today, no doubt about that. She put them on a silver tray and added a plate of cream biscuits, which she could cheerfully have sprinkled with rat poison. She hoped they choked on them.

When everything was ready, she took the tray into the office, just in time to hear Amanda say, "Seven-thirty tomorrow will be fine. Daddy bought me a dress in Paris. I know you're going to love it."

Bryce nodded for Caroline to place the tray on his desk.

"Would you like me to pour?" Her months of training as his secretary allowed her to speak normally, instead of screaming and scratching the other woman's eyes out.

"I'll pour," Amanda cut in. "Bryce likes me doing things for him, don't you, darling?"

Feeling nauseous, Caroline left them ogling each other. She banged away in a frenzy at her typewriter. About fifteen minutes later they came out of his office. Caroline immediately noticed that Bryce's hair was mussed and he had a lipstick smear on his mouth.

"Oh, darling, you've got lippy on your mouth. Let me clean it off. What will your little secretary think?" Amanda took out a white lace handkerchief. Standing closer than necessary, she made a big production of wiping away the offending mark.

Caroline forced herself to continue typing despite the excruciating pain in her heart.

"I'll walk you to your car," Bryce offered, when Amanda stepped back from him. With his hand resting on her waist, they disappeared into the corridor.

****

Two weeks passed. Bryce dated Amanda continuously. If she wasn't in his office, she was on the phone demanding to speak to him. Her arrogance and unmitigated cheek were incredible. She told Bryce that Caroline treated her rudely, and Caroline subsequently suffered a tongue-lashing from him, along with the veiled threat that if she weren't careful her services would be terminated. How unjust. She sobbed the story out to Kerry the night it happened.

"Quit," Kerry snapped. "Leave the pig in the lurch."

Dear God, it was tempting, but she couldn't do it. Seeing Bryce with Amanda was torture—not seeing him at all would be even worse. She must be a masochist who enjoyed self-flagellation and martyrdom.

Andy wrote, saying he had graduated and was now waiting for a permanent posting. She desperately hoped it would be in Victoria, because she needed him now, more than ever before. What if the government wanted him to serve in Vietnam? She shuddered just thinking about it. Dennisons and war didn't mix. There always seemed to be a bullet with their name written on it.

****

On several occasions Bryce had Caroline arrange for flowers to be sent to Amanda. She liked long-stemmed yellow roses. Caroline felt like ordering poison ivy. Amanda had started hinting that she would soon be Mrs. Bryce Harrington.

A week before Christmas, Harrington Constructions gave their annual work Christmas party. It was being held at Alexander Harrington's Toorak mansion and would take the form of a pool party cum barbeque. All members of staff and their partners were invited.

Four of the girls from the typing pool didn't have partners. Caroline arranged to go with them, although she would catch a cab home. One of the girls, Judith, volunteered to drive.

All the staff received a generous bonus, so she splurged on a new outfit. She needed something to cheer herself up. Not that Bryce would notice her with the luscious Amanda sticking to him like a leech. Caroline lived in hope that the other woman wouldn't be attending, because if they met face to face at a social function she would be hard-pressed not to tell Amanda exactly what she thought of her.

A couple of days before the party, Caroline, who now perused the social columns of the newspapers with avid interest, particularly the engagement column, read that the entire Cleveland family, mother, father and daughter, would be flying to Fiji to stay with friends for a few days.

"Imagine flying all that way, paying out heaps of money, just for a couple of days. It stinks," Kerry raged. "Those wealthy types make me sick. Wasting money jaunting around the world, while twenty-year-olds get conscripted into the army."

Caroline laughed. Kerry's political persuasion verged on the communistic. She agreed with her friend, though. Such frivolous waste and self-indulgence was uncalled for, with soldiers dying in Vietnam and civilians being forced out of their homes because of the war.

She rarely mentioned Bryce to Kerry anymore, knowing how her friend detested him. It continued to be one of the only two subjects they couldn't agree on.

The other, of course, was the war in Vietnam. The once-peaceful demonstrations were becoming violent. Protesters were being dragged away by the police, innocent bystanders attacked. Troublemakers had infiltrated the ranks of genuine protesters. The whole situation had become a powder keg, and Kerry and Trevor were sitting right on top of it. Because of Andy's commitment to the army, Caroline didn't want to be close by when it went off.

Chapter 8

On the Friday night of the Christmas party, Caroline rushed home from work to get ready. She had made arrangements to meet the other girls at six o'clock outside work because it was the most central place to congregate. Kerry, who was going to a work party with Trevor, would be staying the night with his parents.

"I won't be home until late Saturday, Caro. Do you think you'll be all right? Trevor's grandparents live in the country, and we're going up on Saturday for the day, so we won't get back until late."

"I'll be fine. Don't worry. I'll keep all the doors and windows locked and not let in any strange men." Caroline grinned. "I promise."

Kerry wore an after-five dress for her Christmas function, as it was a formal affair. Trevor had promised to drop Caroline off at work so she could meet up with the other girls—the dateless and desperate, as they jokingly called themselves.

Caroline wore a pale blue toweling frock with shoestring straps. It had floral appliqués around the hemline. High-heeled white sandals gave her added height. She was tall for a woman, just a fraction over five feet six inches.

She combed her hair, pleased to notice it was already sun-bleached to a shade or two lighter than normal, with blonde streaks scattered through it. She allowed herself a full fringe and parted her hair down the middle, drawing it back from her face by flicking it behind her ears so she could show off her gold stud earrings.

"You look terrific, far too pretty to be eating your heart out over a selfish brute like Harrington. Promise Aunty Kerry that if you meet someone nice at the party, someone who wants to take you home, you'll let him."

Caroline laughed. "I won't promise, but maybe I will. I'm fighting a losing battle anyway."

Trevor arrived to pick them up, and he whistled his approval.

"Good thing I'm not taking you both to the party, I'd be fighting blokes off all night."

Arms linked, Kerry and Trevor left the apartment, Caroline following a step or two behind them, and when they got to the car, she sat in the back.

As they pulled up to the Harrington building, Trevor turned around. "I've been thinking. I could pick you up from the barbeque and you could spend the night at my place. Kerry's worried about you staying on your own, especially with that spate of burglaries in the neighborhood. You could come to my grandparents', too."

"Thanks Trevor, but I'll be all right." She opened the car door. "Go off and enjoy yourselves. Don't worry about me. I'm a big girl now."

When she alighted from the car outside of work, the other girls were already waiting.

On arrival at the Harrington mansion, Judith parked the car out in the street, and they all walked together through a pair of enormous iron gates set into a bluestone wall.

A uniformed security guard escorted them to the pool area. *Probably making sure we don't trespass into the house,* Caroline thought. She would have given up a year's pay just to have one tiny peek inside the place where Bryce had spent his childhood.

The expansive grounds were lit with hurricane lanterns that illuminated the gardens and threw a soft mantle of light around the numerous trees and shrubs.

The poolside area was paved with cobblestones. A huge barbeque had been set up at one end and, judging by the appetizing aromas emanating from it, the meat was already cooking.

Caroline smiled at several people she knew from work before Harrington Senior claimed her attention.

"How are you this evening, my dear?" As always whenever they met, he stared at her intently. Never rude, of course, too much of a gentleman for that, but his eyes took on a contemplative puzzlement. Did he suspect how she felt about his son?

"I'm fine, thanks. You've chosen a perfect night for a

barbeque, Mr. Harrington."

"We have, haven't we?" He rubbed his hands together. "If you would excuse me, I'll see how the food is coming along." He headed towards the pool area. No sign of Bryce. Perhaps he wasn't coming. She didn't know whether to be glad or sorry.

A waiter hovering at her elbow asked what she wanted to drink.

"Um, I'm not sure. What have you got?"

"The fruit punch is nice, Miss. And there's sparkling wine, beer..."

"Fruit punch, thanks," she cut him off.

She accepted a glass and took a sip. It tasted delicious and would quench her thirst. She wasn't into drinking much alcohol.

Long tables, set up at one side of the pool, were covered with various salads and other delicacies, a virtual banquet.

Judith came up to Caroline. "Enjoying yourself? The Harringtons always put on a good turn. Santa will be coming soon."

"Santa!"

"Yes, it's a Harrington Christmas party tradition. We always get a nice present."

At that moment, a voice rang out. "Ho, ho, ho, Merry Christmas, everyone."

Caroline could scarcely believe her eyes. Bryce was dressed up in a Santa suit, with bushy white whiskers flowing halfway down his chest.

He sat himself down on a chair and dumped his sack on the ground. "Have you all been good little girls and boys?"

Caroline found herself first in line.

"Have you been a good girl? Come and sit on Santa's knee."

With everyone cheering her on, she couldn't refuse even if she'd wanted to.

"Yes, I've been good, Santa." She perched on his knee, resting one hand on his shoulder. She couldn't resist the urge to stare into his face. His eyes were a clear, sparkling gray tonight.

"Can Santa have a kiss?" he whispered in her ear,

and she felt her cheeks grow hot.

"No, sorry." She shook her head for emphasis.

"Oh well, here you are. Merry Christmas." He handed her an envelope.

"Thank you, Santa, Merry Christmas." She forced herself to get off his knee so the next girl in the line could take her place.

"No, you can't sit on Santa's knee," Bryce told a grinning young man who followed the girl. "Only pretty young ladies get that privilege."

"Oh, Santa, I'm crushed."

"Too bad," Santa replied with a chuckle.

Caroline noticed that everyone received the same-sized envelope. When she opened hers, she discovered a twelve-month free pass to any Melbourne drive-in or movie theatre.

Santa's visit broke the ice, and everyone started laughing and talking as they got into the festive spirit.

Several of the girls headed towards the pool. At their insistence, Caroline slipped out of her frock, glad that Judith had told her to wear her bathers underneath. Swimming was one activity she loved. Without vanity, she knew she was good. At school, the swimming coach used to tell her that if she took private lessons after school hours, she might make the Olympic training squad.

Her mother couldn't afford the extra tuition fee. She battled to pay the school fees for her and Andy as it was. If they hadn't received a special grant from the school trustees because they were the children of a former pupil, they wouldn't have been able to attend such a prestigious school.

Caroline dived into the pool, where a number of Harrington employees were enjoying the water. She glided through the water, reveling in the liquid coolness against her skin. What bliss! No wonder the rich and famous guarded their lifestyle so tenaciously.

She executed a perfect tumble turn before heading back towards the other end of the pool, oblivious to anything but the magic feel of the water. She did several more lengths before she realized everyone else had left the pool. Glancing up she saw that they were all lined up watching her.

When she came up out of the water, everyone cheered, and she felt so embarrassed she didn't know where to look. Scurrying towards her clothes, she was waylaid by Alexander Harrington.

"Wonderful exhibition, my dear. Where did you learn to swim so well?"

"At school. I...I didn't realize anyone was watching. I tend to forget everything once I hit the water."

"I didn't know you could swim so well." Bryce joined his father. "Have you had much coaching?"

"I did at school. My coach thought I was okay."

"I'll bet he did." He stepped back a pace and let his gaze wander all over her, and once more she felt a hot rush of color to her cheeks.

Bryce was now dressed in beige shorts with a brown, short-sleeved polo shirt. She tried not to stare at his sandaled feet and tanned, well-muscled legs.

"What would you like to drink?" His devastating white-toothed smile gave her goosebumps. With a hand resting lightly on her shoulder, he steered her towards the drink waiter.

"Fruit punch, thanks. This will be my second one. I hope it isn't alcoholic."

He laughed. "It's only fruit juice, with a few strawberries floating around to make it look more exotic."

Handing her a glass of the punch, he took a beer for himself.

"I should put my dress back on." She couldn't help but notice his intense scrutiny. Remembering the last time they were alone, she wanted to cover herself as quickly as possible.

"You're still wet. Besides, heaps of people are wearing bathers. It's a pool party, for goodness sake." He took a mouthful of beer. "I'd like a swim myself, but..."

"But it wouldn't do to rub shoulders with the workers?"

"Are you accusing me of being a snob?" His arctic tones could have frozen water.

"Aren't you?" She wondered why she wanted to provoke him, knowing how hot-tempered he could be.

He hesitated for a moment. "No, I don't think I'm a snob. In fact," his lips twisted into a sneer, "I enjoy rubbing shoulders with my workers. Some more than others, of course."

Before she realized his intention, he drew her into a darkened corner of the garden, where they were shielded from the others by a rose-covered trellis. His mouth came down on hers, hard and angry. It was a punishing kiss, and he crushed her so tightly against him she feared she might suffocate. But—what bliss!

He forced her mouth open with his impatient, thrusting tongue and a sudden surge of electric current shot through her. He must have felt her almost instantaneous capitulation, because the kisses changed. They became gentle, sensuous, working her mouth until it trembled and opened eagerly to receive his tribute.

He kissed her eyelids, her throat and shoulders. When she felt him untying the halter neck of her bikini top, she didn't care. This was Bryce, the only man she would ever love. Nothing else mattered except him, now and always.

His impatient hands slid her bikini top down and his mouth found her nipple. He drew her breasts together and suckled both nipples until they became aroused and super-sensitive. Excitement swirled in frenzied, turbulent waves deep within her womanly recess as he drew the rosy tips even deeper into his hot mouth. She was certain this was as near to paradise as she would ever get on earth.

Finally he raised his head. "My God, what are you doing to me?"

He started moving his body slowly, sensuously against hers.

"Let's get out of here and go somewhere more private," he whispered.

But before she could frame an answer they heard Alexander Harrington calling out.

Bryce cursed under his breath. He moved quickly towards his father, giving Caroline time to adjust her bikini top.

"It's time to eat, son. What on earth are you doing out here?"

"Caroline and I were discussing a work matter."

"For goodness sake, this isn't the time or the place to

be discussing business."

Caroline came up to them, glad that the darkness hid her face from the older man. "I am starting to feel hungry. Must be the night air." She wondered how she could speak after being kissed so thoroughly by Bryce.

"Well, come along. The steaks are getting cold. I've been looking for you for more than five minutes."

She followed the two men to where the cook was barbecuing steak and sausages. A number of people who had already received their meat were congregated around a large table, helping themselves to an assortment of salads.

"Steak, Caroline?" Bryce asked, in a voice that sounded almost normal.

"Just a small piece, thanks." She didn't feel like eating. She *was* starving, but only for Bryce and the passion his kisses promised. She walked a tightrope to danger, but didn't care. For once in her life she wasn't going to be cautious, sensible Caroline Dennison.

She watched in amazement as a fat, juicy T-bone landed on her plate.

"If that's a small piece, I'd hate to try a big one." She smiled at Bryce as he helped himself to a large T-bone and a couple of sausages.

He picked up one miniature bread roll for each of them.

"I'll let you serve yourself the salad," he said.

She followed him around the table, helping herself to coleslaw, lettuce and tomato. There were jars of what looked like tiny black balls. Probably caviar, she surmised.

She wandered over to where several deck chairs were set up and found a vacant one close to the pool. Bryce followed and sat next to her.

They didn't speak while they ate their food. "Who did you come with?" he asked.

"I met a group of girls outside work, and we came together. I'll get a cab home."

"No. I'll take you."

"Thanks, but I couldn't take you out of your way. You'd have to come all the way back here again."

"I'm staying at my own place. You should have asked

me to give you a lift home."

"I didn't have the nerve."

"Am I such an ogre? Don't answer that." He gave a deep rich chuckle that did funny things to her insides.

"I wasn't going to, on the grounds it might incriminate me." Laughter gave a lilt to her voice. This was how it should be, laughing, teasing, enjoying each other's company.

When they'd finished eating, Bryce took their plates over to the table. "Come and have some dessert," he said on his return, grasping her hands and pulling her up.

There was fresh fruit salad, huge bowls of whipped cream, mud cake and strawberry pavlova. After they'd filled their plates Bryce picked up a bottle of champagne and a couple of glasses. He poured champagne into the two crystal goblets and handed one to her as soon as she was seated.

"Merry Christmas, Caroline."

"Thanks. Same to you." They clinked glasses. Between mouthfuls of dessert, intermittently washed down with champagne, they discussed the Test cricket.

"For a female you know a lot about cricket."

"My brother used to play, so I went to a few games with him. I saw a couple of the Tests between Australia and England. I just love the atmosphere. Everyone in their shorts and thongs, the guys loaded down with car fridges full of beer. There was even a streaker at one of the matches." She laughed at the happy memories. She couldn't remember when she had last felt so carefree.

"I'll just take our glasses back. Won't be long." Bryce stood and moved towards the table. Within a short time he was striding back towards her, moving with a loose-limbed grace. She would never tire of watching him. He sat down next to her and draped his arm across her shoulders.

"You don't speak much about your family," he finally said, as if he felt the need to break the silence between them.

"I've only got a brother now," she said with a catch in her voice. "My parents are both dead."

"I'm sorry." He genuinely sounded like he was. "It must be lonely for you. Do you see much of your brother?"

"No, but we're close."

As the night wore on, some of the guests started drifting away. Just before midnight Bryce suggested they should leave, also. Caroline had consumed several glasses of champagne and felt happy. In fact, she was slightly muzzy in the head, but happy—ecstatically happy because she was with Bryce.

"I'm dropping Caroline off on my way home," he told his father when they bid the old man goodbye. She was glad Bryce hadn't forgotten his promise to take her home.

"Thank you for inviting me, Mr. Harrington. It was a great party," Caroline told him with sincerity.

"That's all right. Glad you enjoyed it. I think everything went off well, don't you, son?"

"Yes, as always." Bryce draped his arm across his father's shoulders, and Caroline felt moved by the obvious affection between the two men.

Chapter 9

Bryce held Caroline's hand as they strolled towards the Jaguar, parked in front of an enormous garage. This would have to be one of the best nights in her whole life.

He had spent a lot of time with her, so perhaps he did feel something special for her. The champagne had gone to her head, making her reckless, and it urged her to throw caution to the wind.

"I'd like to go to your place for coffee," she announced after they had been driving for a short time. This might be her only chance to see where he lived, but more importantly, she wanted to savor his company for as long as possible.

"I'm not sure that would be a good idea."

"Just a quick cup of coffee, unless you don't trust me," she taunted.

"It's not you I don't trust. You're playing with fire."

"Please." She reached out and caressed his cheek. "I've had such a wonderful time. I don't want it to end yet."

"You're very sweet. I wish..." He gave a deep sigh.

"What do you wish?"

"Oh, forget it."

Settling back in the comfortable seat, she felt her eyes growing heavy. She shouldn't have guzzled so much champagne. She awoke with a jolt when the car stopped in a basement car park. They must be at his place.

"We're here, sleepyhead." He laughed softly as he locked his door and came around to the passenger side to help her out and lock the passenger door. His arm draped across her shoulders, they headed towards an elevator to take them up to his apartment.

They got out on the tenth floor, where Caroline followed him down a carpeted corridor to a door he unlocked and pushed open to usher her in. There was a dimmer on the light switch, she realized, when a subdued glow enveloped the room.

"Have a seat while I put the percolator on. I could do with a coffee—it might clear my head."

Caroline sat on the velour couch, sinking gratefully into its softness. Her legs were weak; her whole body felt fluid, as if she were floating on a calm sea.

She forced her wavering vision to view the room. White shag pile carpet covered the floor. It was a beautiful room but somehow lacking in warmth.

Bryce returned with two ceramic coffee mugs. "White with one sugar, isn't it?" He cocked an eyebrow.

"Yes, thank you."

They sipped the coffee in silence, and Caroline's head began to clear. What a fool she had been to drink so much champagne when she wasn't used to it. When she'd finished her coffee, he took the empty mug and placed it on the coffee table.

He put his arm around her to draw her close and the subtle scent of his aftershave lotion infused her nostrils, causing her to become lightheaded again.

"Did you enjoy the party?"

"Yes, it was great." *But this is the best part of all*, she thought happily. She had him to herself, if only for a short time.

He kissed her, gently, almost hesitantly at first. This was madness, but she returned his kisses with passion. Trying to tell him with actions what she couldn't tell him in words. She loved him.

He eased her back onto the couch until she lay stretched out along the length of it.

His hands caressed her breasts through her frock and she trembled at his touch. She wanted to feel his hands on her bare flesh. Wanted him to see her blossoming nipples. She wore her bikini bottoms but not the top. Without being asked, she slipped her dress up over her head. His strangled groan seemed to echo around the room.

He shifted slightly so his body covered hers. His mouth devoured her lips, her throat, her eyelids. "Oh, God," he gasped the words out. "I want you so badly it's killing me."

He dragged off his shirt. The touch of his bare, hair-roughened chest against her breasts became an exquisite form of torture. Her womanly center pulsated with an urgency that matched his.

He rained kisses from her breasts to her navel, and when she felt his hands go to the tie of her bikini briefs she was beyond caring about anything except him.

"Will you stay the night with me?" he asked in a voice raw with emotion.

"Yes. I love you." She was shocked when the last three words fell out of her mouth of their own volition.

"Prove it. Stay the night with me."

Effortlessly he picked her up. Cradling her in his arms, he strode to his bedroom and laid her on the bed.

His mouth covered hers. His hands stroked her heated skin, fanning a passion she had never known existed until he brought it into raging life.

When he eased himself away, she could hear him removing his clothing in the darkness. He was naked when he joined her on the bed.

His hand slid between her thighs and caressed her soft, feminine curls. She raised her knees, letting her legs fall open to give him easy access. He parted her quivering flesh with his thumbs. She felt his tongue slide into her hot moistness. He suckled her bud, tugging it gently with his teeth, taking it into his warm mouth, working her until she was demented with need.

She heard his harsh rapid breathing, or maybe it was her own. His shoulders were damp with perspiration by the time he entered her feminine recess with one long, powerful thrust.

For an agonized second she felt a tearing pain, followed by ecstasy as they moved together in a passionate frenzy. She had never been with a man before, but instinctively knew how to give and receive pleasure beyond anything she had dreamed possible before. She cried out when Bryce brought her to an earth-shattering climax. A million stars exploded inside her head, the light so bright she was momentarily blinded.

He didn't move away from her, just kissed away the salty tears she didn't even realize she had shed.

"I'm sorry." He wrapped his arms around her. "I didn't realize. Did I hurt you?"

"No, it was wonderful. I love you so much. You love

me just a little, don't you?"

He didn't answer, but by this time she felt too drowsy to notice as she floated on a cloud of after-sex euphoria.

Bryce felt cold-stone sober now. "Shit." His head throbbed. He never drank champagne as a rule, because it gave him a headache. Not that he had consumed all that many glasses anyway, but mixed with the couple of whiskies he'd shared with his father before the party, and two or three beers, it had proved a deadly combination. He was a bloody fool even to have gotten behind the wheel of a car, let alone to have taken Caroline to his apartment.

He rolled away from her, feeling sick with remorse, now his passion had cooled and he realized the ramifications of what might follow. The regrets, the tears and recriminations. Caroline had given him something special tonight, and he wasn't a worthy recipient of such a gift. The women he used for lovemaking were experienced. He cursed his stupidity for not having realized sooner, but it was the Sixties, for God's sake, free love and all that.

His head pounded, so he climbed out of bed and wandered into his bathroom. Fumbling around in the medicine cabinet, he found some pain-killing tablets and swallowed a couple with a mouthful of water.

Back in the bedroom Caroline still slept, and he slid carefully into bed to avoid waking her. He wasn't looking forward to facing her in the cold light of day. He was in no fit state to drive now, and he couldn't wake her up and bundle her into a cab. That would be too crass. She wasn't a call girl, and he would never treat her like one.

Next morning, as Bryce woke, he felt something warm and soft lying against him. Last night's events came flooding back with shocking intensity. In the morning light she looked young, vulnerable, but oh, so beautiful. Her cheeks were still stained with tears, her well-shaped lips puckered. The sheet, having dropped away, left her creamy breasts and rosy nipples exposed.

His breath caught in his throat and once more he felt a fiery surge of desire. What was the matter with him? His excuse for seducing her last night had been that too much alcohol had impaired his judgment. There was no excuse for his carnal thoughts now. It was sheer, rampant lust.

He slid out of bed before he gave in to his urges and made wild, passionate love to her again. By the time he'd finished showering and shaving, he at least felt physically better, but emotionally he couldn't expunge the guilt of what he had done. With a towel draped around his hips, he padded across to his dressing room, where he dressed in jeans and a burgundy polo shirt. Caroline was still asleep, so he tiptoed out to the sitting room.

Their discarded clothing lay in tangled confusion on the couch and the floor. He put his in the soiled linen basket, took hers into the bedroom and laid them across the dressing table.

He made his way to the kitchen. He was not domesticated. Didn't have to be, when there was hired staff around. He could cook the bare essentials and make a decent cup of coffee.

Glancing at the wall clock, he realized it was nine o'clock. Hell. After making some coffee and toast, he arranged it on a wooden tray and took it into the bedroom.

"Caroline," he lowered his voice when he spoke her name, but it still penetrated her sleep. As she opened her eyes he noticed bewilderment, followed by a strawberry flush staining her cheeks and throat.

"I...I made you some breakfast."

Caroline stared at Bryce without speaking and started to sit up. Oh, God, what had she done? She made a desperate grab for the sheet and pulled it up over her bare breasts. She didn't know where to look or what to say.

He put the tray on the bedside table. "The bathroom is through there. After you've eaten, you might like a shower. There are plenty of fresh towels in the cupboard under the vanity basin. Use my dressing gown, if you like." His words were stilted. He pointed to the navy silk robe lying across the foot of the bed. "I'll be in the kitchen. Call out if you need anything." He turned and left the room.

Caroline raised herself higher in the bed, wrapping the sheet under her arms. If she ate anything she would be ill, but she drank the coffee. What had she done? Shame and humiliation engulfed her.

She loved Bryce, loved him so much it had become a burning, tormenting flame scorching right through her, but even at the height of his passion he had mentioned nothing about love.

She drank the coffee in a couple of gulps. It burned her throat, but she welcomed the diversion the pain gave. He didn't love her, probably didn't even like her overmuch. Fueled by alcohol, she had encouraged him, thrown away her inhibitions, and he had been the same. The only reasonable course of action now was to try to make a dignified exit.

Slipping out of bed, she donned the robe. It felt smooth against her skin, and his male scent lingered in the fibers. Should she make the bed? She swung around, and her hands flew to her face in horror. The pristine whiteness of his sheet was stained with droplets of her virginal blood. Oh, God. She started trembling. What now? Change the sheets? Ask him what to do?

She folded her arms across her breasts and rocked backwards and forwards. After the initial pain of his penetration, there had been only bliss. Bryce was too consummate a lover to leave her feeling sore. No, the stark truth of what she gave away last night screamed at her from the bed linen.

If he had loved her, those droplets of blood would have been a badge of honor. She rushed over to the bed, wrenched the sheets off and stormed into the bathroom. By the time she disposed of the linen in his washing basket, her spurt of anger had fizzled out.

In normal circumstances she would have admired the opulent black marble bath. Two people could stretch out fully in it. But for all she cared right now, it could have been a horse trough. Discarding the robe, she stepped into the shower cubicle. There were two sets of shower knobs. His and hers?

She turned the taps on full bore, wishing she could stay there forever. Eventually she stepped out and, after drying herself on a large fluffy towel, stood trembling, prolonging the time until she would have to confront Bryce.

She folded the towel in half, hung it on the rack, and went out into his bedroom. Her clothes had been laid out on the dressing table, and she slipped them on. Where were her shoes? Probably still in the sitting room where she had kicked them off last night. Her bra and panties were in her handbag. Thank goodness he hadn't had to handle such intimate items of clothing.

Caroline picked up a tan leather brush and ran it through her hair. Grimacing at her wan appearance, she took in several deep steadying breaths. She could do this. She had to. Mustering her courage, she slowly walked into the kitchen.

Bryce lounged at an island-type bench, reading the papers. An empty plate and cup sat next to him.

"I wasn't hungry." She placed the tray on the bench.

When he glanced up she saw that the well-shaped lips she had tasted so wantonly last night were drawn into tight lines—still extremely kissable, though.

"Another cup of coffee?" he asked in overly polite tones.

"Yes, thank you."

He switched the percolator back on and sat watching her without speaking.

He cleared his throat a couple of times. "I'm sorry about last night. I know it's inadequate, but what else can I say?"

"It wasn't your fault. I shouldn't have asked to come here. I should have stopped you before, well, before things got out of control." Her voice wobbled. If only he said he loved her, everything would be all right. She would be happy instead of distraught.

He didn't say anything more, just turned the percolator off when it bubbled, and refilled both their cups.

They drank in silence. She idly noticed a modern wall oven with concealed hot plates. There was a dishwasher and garbage disposal unit. Everything looked ultramodern and expensive, but cold and clinical.

When the silence became unbearable, she broke it by saying, "I'd like to go home soon. Could you call me a cab?"

"I'll run you home when we've finished our coffee."

"I...I took off the bed linen and..."

"You shouldn't have bothered," he said, cutting her off. "My housekeeper comes in on a daily basis and takes care of everything."

Not bloodstained sheets, she thought, feeling sick to her stomach.

He gave a tight smile. He looked embarrassed, but he couldn't feel as bad as she did.

When she finished her coffee, she put the cup down and stood up.

"I'd like to leave now, please."

He glanced down at his bare feet. "I'll just go and put some shoes on."

She waited for him in the sitting room. Daylight only emphasized the luxurious surroundings, and she realized Bryce's world could never be hers. Not that the realization could stifle the love and longing in her heart. Insurmountable obstacles could be overcome by love, but he didn't love her, pure and simple.

He drove her home without speaking. She glanced at his stony, brooding profile a couple of times. It didn't take much imagination on her part to realize she wasn't the only one regretting last night's passion. He pulled up outside her apartment and came around to let her out of the car.

"Will you be all right?" he mumbled when they reached her door.

"Yes, thank you."

"I'm sorry again for what happened last night. If I could undo the damage I've done, I would." He spoke slowly, almost warily, and she wondered whether he thought she might abuse him, break down or go into screaming hysterics. Of course, she wouldn't allow herself the luxury, yet. But if he offered her money, she'd scream the place down.

She inserted her key in the lock.

"Goodbye, Caroline." He ran his finger gently across her trembling lips.

"Goodbye." Blinking back tears, she watched him walk away. Once inside the apartment she broke down completely, crying until she was exhausted. Her head ached so badly, she feared it might split open. After gulping down a couple of painkillers, she crawled into bed.

Caroline woke to the sounds of Kerry and Trevor's laughter. How could they laugh, she thought bleakly. She'd never be able to laugh again. She was sick with shame and remorse. Bryce might be a mature, experienced man, but she was equally culpable—more so, if she were honest. She was the one who had suggested they go to his apartment.

She'd known the dangers. What man could refuse such a blatant sexual invitation? He would have assumed he was dealing with an experienced woman. Probably thought she was easy, promiscuous, like many of her age group, into free love and damn the consequences.

She valued her reputation and morality. It lay in tatters now, though. The sensible, if cowardly, way out would be to ring up Bryce on Monday and say she wouldn't be coming in anymore. Being a masochist, she couldn't do it. Of course, he might fire her to save himself from embarrassment.

"We're home, Caroline." Kerry danced into the bedroom. At least she had enjoyed her weekend. "Did you have a good time at the party?"

"Yes, terrific. Bryce drove me home. I don't feel up to talking now, sorry. I've got a shocking headache."

"We're off for some Chinese food. Like me to get you some?"

"No, thanks, I couldn't." The thought of food was nauseating. If she never ate again, it would be too soon. She stayed in bed. It was easier than facing Kerry when she came back.

Chapter 10

On Monday morning when the alarm went off, Caroline wanted to stay in bed forever. The mere thought of facing Bryce gave her palpitations. She dressed in a bright tangerine dress in the hope it might add some color to her wan appearance. A touch of liquid makeup camouflaged the ravages caused by a weekend of weeping.

Kerry didn't comment on her paleness but kept giving her long, speculative looks over the breakfast table. To save her life, Caroline couldn't have told her friend about Friday night. She felt too ashamed.

She caught the bus to work, went through the glass doors and up in the elevator without seeing anyone, thank goodness. When she entered her office, she noticed that Bryce wasn't in yet. Switching on the power to her typewriter, she started typing out the memo left over from Friday. It needed to be circulated around the building, notifying staff that the firm would be closing down on Christmas Eve and resuming on the second of January.

Four more days to go. Then she would have a week off to lick her wounds. She prayed for the strength to carry on until Christmas Eve. Bryce came in a short while afterwards.

"Good morning, Caroline. How are you feeling today?" He stopped beside her desk.

"I'm all right, thanks." She didn't raise her head, too embarrassed to even glance at him.

He hovered for a moment before striding into his own office.

The buzzer sounded about ten minutes later. Gathering up her pad and pencil, she took a couple of steadying breaths and headed for his office. She could do this. She had to do it if she wanted to keep her job. It was as simple as that. She rapped on the door and walked in before her courage deserted her.

Bryce was sprawled out in his chair, one foot resting

on his desk, but he swung his foot down the minute he saw her. She took her usual chair opposite him and sat with her head bowed as if studying her shorthand notebook.

She felt his gaze on her, but didn't look up. A taut silence hung between them. Tangible, embarrassing.

He cleared his throat and she raised her head. "I've several letters to dictate. After that, if you could get Geoff Davies to come in here, please, I've decided to take a few weeks off. I need a break." She watched a ghost of a smile flit across his handsome face. He gave her another long, considering stare before starting to dictate.

She finished several letters and one long report.

"That's the lot, thanks."

She scuttled back to her office. He hadn't specifically mentioned Friday night, thank goodness. But what could he say? I'm sorry for having sex with you? And the worst part was that it had been just sex. Love didn't come into the equation, as far as he was concerned.

She worked hard all day, stopping only for a quick lunch break. Mr. Davies came in to see Bryce, and they were closeted together for over an hour.

At long last it was time to leave for home. Never in her whole life had she felt so relieved to see the end of a day.

****

For the next four days Caroline ate, slept and went to work like a robot. Bryce became his usual unpredictable self. He snapped at her on several occasions. Obviously, as far as he was concerned, Friday night never happened. Of course it would be different for a man, particularly one who lived by the twin mottoes of "Variety is the spice of life" and "Love them and leave them."

On the last day of work, Amanda Cleveland minced in.

"I want to see Bryce."

Her canary yellow silk dress had a matching jacket. A wide-brimmed straw hat covered her dark curls. She looked decked out for a day at the races.

"Mr. Harrington might be busy," Caroline began, but Amanda brushed her off.

"He'll see me." She swept past like a yacht in full sail

and went into the office, slamming the door behind her. She came back about fifteen minutes later with a self-satisfied smirk, like a greedy cat that had just lapped up a saucer of rich, fresh cream.

"Oh, that man is absolutely devastating," she commented to Caroline. It was the only time Amanda ever spoke to her in a civilized tone.

Amanda had returned with a vengeance. Was she good in bed? Of course. Bryce wouldn't bother with her otherwise—or would he? They both came from wealthy, privileged backgrounds, the *crème de la crème* of Melbourne society.

Bryce came out about half an hour later. "Would you order some flowers for Miss Cleveland, please. The usual. Oh, and get some for yourself, whatever you like." He strolled back into his own office. How incredibly cruel! Caroline's heart felt as if it had been shredded by a razor. How could a man make love to a woman less than a week ago, then get this same woman to send flowers to his latest fancy? Worse still, offhandedly tell her to order some for herself. That really made her blood boil. *I'll have to leave here. No way can I endure such purgatory.*

When Bryce returned from his holiday she would hand in her resignation. Was Amanda going away with him? It was devastating to think so. Caroline would have preferred to be gone before he got back, but many firms closed over December and January, and few employers would be willing to put on extra staff at this time of year.

She couldn't afford to be out of work. There was no future here now, only the three 'h' words—hurt, heartbreak and humiliation. Amanda had unwittingly given her the courage to leave.

They finished work early on Christmas Eve, and some of the staff were congregating at a nearby hotel for a Christmas drink. She didn't want to go but couldn't think of a reasonable excuse to get out of it. A few of the other bosses attended, but not Bryce. It was the only decent break she'd had all week. Caroline ordered a gin squash and sat down next to Mr. Davies to drink it.

"I hope you have a Merry Christmas," he said sincerely.

"Thanks, I hope you do, too. Also your family."

This would be the worst Christmas she had ever put in. It went without saying.

"Is everything all right?" He sounded genuinely concerned.

"Yes, of course. Like everyone else, I just need a break," she lied. Lying had become second nature to her now, and she was getting quite good at it.

"I'm looking forward to working with you after the holidays. Bryce has filled me in on everything, so I don't think we'll have too many problems." He gave one of his charming smiles, and she felt terrible, knowing she planned to leave him in the lurch.

They were a cheerful crowd at the hotel. With a second drink under her belt, she joined in on the merriment to a certain extent. Finally, wishing each other the compliments of the season, they drifted out into the street and went their separate ways.

****

When Caroline arrived home, Andy was there with his cheerful "Hi!"

She dashed up to him, flung her arms around his neck and kissed him on the cheek. "You can't know how pleased I am to see you."

"Wow, what a welcome. I'm happy to see you, too."

"Look." Kerry pushed her way between the two of them. "Do you like it? She waved her hand about.

"You're engaged?" Caroline squealed. "Oh, congratulations." She hugged her friend, happy to see her so ecstatic.

"She nagged me into it." Trevor grinned.

"Yeah, I'll bet she did, mate." Andy slapped him on the back. "We need a drink to celebrate."

They found some lemonade and toasted each other. "To the happy couple," Andy said, and they clinked their glasses together.

"Merry Christmas and a happy and prosperous New Year," Kerry yelled out.

Caroline couldn't stop a little twinge of envy as she looked into Kerry's excited face. It made the future stretching before Caroline seem even bleaker than ever. No job. No Bryce. What kind of masochist could love a man who treated her with such contempt?

"Are you okay?" Andy stared into her face. "You're looking washed out."

"I'm all right. Just been working too hard."

"Bryce Harrington is an ungrateful slave driver. He didn't even give you a Christmas present," Kerry raged. "After all you've done for him."

"Everyone got a movie voucher."

"That was from the company, not him."

"It doesn't worry me." It was a lie. It hurt that he hadn't bothered to buy her a gift. "Take some money out of petty cash and buy yourself something for Christmas," he had said. She didn't want anything from petty cash. She wanted something from him. She was a fool.

"Anyway, I've decided to leave Harringtons."

"Good for you." Kerry clapped her hands. "You're wasting your time and talent there. Arrogant bastard doesn't appreciate you. Wait until he realizes how much work you took off his hands. No one else would put up with his crap. Serve him right," Kerry finished off viciously.

****

The four of them spent Boxing Day together at the beach. Caroline wore her bikini, but she hated it now. She vowed to buy a new one as soon as she could afford it, then take pleasure in throwing this little black number away in the garbage can. It brought back too many bitter memories.

The four of them skylarked about, splashing and duck diving.

Caroline couldn't believe how tanned Andy was. "Remember when we were kids? How we used to burn?" she said. "Mum always yelled at you to stay out of the sun."

"Yeah, I know. I suppose it was sensible, us being so fair."

"She didn't care about me." Caroline tried to hide the bitterness in her voice. It wasn't Andy's fault their mother thought he was the golden-haired boy, literally and figuratively.

"It wasn't right. I always knew she favored me, but I didn't realize you noticed it, too."

I would have been blind not to, she almost said. "All

water under the bridge. You're nice and tanned now, though." She ran her finger across his well-muscled shoulders and arms. He was in the peak of physical condition.

"I've been doing a course of weightlifting," he admitted with a grin. "I might need it when I get my posting. It could be Vietnam."

"No!" She wrung her hands. "Oh, God. Not over there."

"Hey, it will be all right. I want to go, but they put you through a pretty rigorous medical first."

She couldn't argue with him. He was an army officer trained to fight, and he would do so. The Australians were sustaining battle casualties now. But she didn't want her brother going to Vietnam, to be killed like all the other Dennisons who went to war.

She enjoyed her day at the beach just so long as she didn't think about either Bryce or the war in Vietnam. Kerry and Trevor's cheerful banter did a lot to revive her flagging spirits. *Maybe I will forget Bryce in time.* Especially once she left Harringtons. Not seeing him all the time might help heal her wounds.

****

Once Andy had returned to the army, she set out on a cleaning frenzy, keeping busy so she wouldn't think of Bryce. While she waited for a load of washing to be ready, she sat down in a lounge chair and flipped through the pages of the daily newspaper. She turned to the society pages and was shocked to see a picture of Bryce. Was that Amanda with him? The picture was fuzzy and the woman stood in the background, but it could have been her. He was leaving for an unknown holiday destination. *A little love nest for two*, she thought bitterly. *I should hate him for what he's putting me through, not love him.* What kind of fool was she?

Kerry only got the main holidays off work, so Caroline spent the next few days alone. How much washing and cleaning could one small apartment stand? God, she needed something to fill in her time other than housework and perusing the papers to see if there were any decent jobs on offer. She hated herself for being so pathetic. If the daytime was bad, nighttime proved a thousand times worse. Lonely, tormented.

She took long walks to a nearby park, went swimming at Elwood Beach a couple of times, but none of it was much fun on her own.

"Why don't you come to Trevor's New Year's party?" Kerry asked.

"No, thanks. You go and enjoy yourself. I'll be all right." Parties were out for a while. In fact, if she didn't go to another party for twenty years, it would be too soon. She had never been a party girl, but now she wanted to be a recluse.

****

Caroline started back at work, feeling better for having had the break. Accidentally glancing into the mirror in her office, she was surprised at her reflection. The trips out in the sun had brought color to her cheeks and bleached her hair completely blonde. Pity Bryce wasn't around to notice the improvement.

"Good morning, Caroline. Did you have a nice Christmas?" Mr. Davies greeted her with a smile.

"Yes, lovely, thanks. What about you?"

"I had a good break. Took the family camping along the foreshore at Rosebud." He chuckled. "I thought you might have commented on my suntan."

"Sorry." She laughed. "I didn't notice."

"Let's get started, shall we? Bryce left a ton of work for us."

They worked well together. Mr. Davies didn't have the quick brilliance of Bryce or his fiery temper. No wonder his secretary, Dulcie, loved her job so much. He dictated slowly, so her outlines were perfect, easy to read back. Not like with Bryce, when she had to concentrate on every word he uttered.

"Well, that's about it, thanks. Take your time about typing them up. There's no great hurry. I'll be out of the office for the rest of the day."

After finishing all Mr. Davies' work, she inserted a piece of plain foolscap paper and started typing out her resignation.

Dear Mr. Harrington,

I am resigning as your secretary. I have been offered a similar position closer to home and, after much

deliberation, I have decided to accept it.
I enjoyed working for you.
Caroline

It sounded stilted, pathetic, but what else could she say? The truth, maybe? *I'm head over heels in love with you and can't stand watching you with other women.* Or, *You made love to me once and I desperately want you to do it again.* Having tasted his passion, there was little likelihood of her finding such rapture again.

She checked her work for any typos, signed it with a sudden defiant flourish, and shoved it into her desk drawer. *I'll wait another few days before I hand it in.* It was no hardship working for Mr. Davies, and the extra money would come in handy.

****

A week before Bryce arrived back, Caroline woke at her usual time for work, jumped up from bed, and the room spun. She grabbed hold of the dressing table to stop her shaky legs from collapsing under her. Nausea filled her throat, and she felt close to vomiting.

Kerry was still asleep, thank goodness. Having to listen to one of her lectures about the dangers of food poisoning would be the absolute end. She staggered into the bathroom and slumped against the wash basin until the sickness abated.

After she'd showered and eaten breakfast, she felt normal again. *Probably picked up some twenty-four-hour tummy bug,* she thought, as she headed to work. Couldn't be anything much, otherwise she would have gotten bus sick.

The next three mornings in a row the same thing happened, but on the fourth morning she vomited.

I've definitely got a gastric virus, she thought as she dragged herself off to work. When she fainted in the elevator, Mr. Davies arranged for her to be sent home in a cab, and she spent the rest of the day in bed. She couldn't remember ever feeling so sick or wretched.

"You're going to see a doctor," Kerry insisted when she arrived home. "You've been looking awful for days. You could end up with full-blown gastroenteritis, if you aren't careful."

"I know. I can't go on like this. When I fainted in the

elevator, it was terrible. I fell almost at Mr. Davies' feet. I don't know who got the biggest shock, him or me." She forced a laugh because Kerry looked so worried. Inwardly, she was a bundle of nerves. If she got really sick and couldn't work, what then?

Caroline fronted up to the doctor's rooms determined to get to the bottom of this mystery illness once and for all. *I won't let him fob me off. I'll insist on blood tests.* She couldn't afford the luxury of messing around with pills or potions.

The doctor was male. He wore a white coat and had a stethoscope slung around his neck. *Like God sitting at the judgment table*, she thought on a note of hysteria.

"Now, Miss, um," he glanced at her card. "Dennison. What do you think is wrong with you?"

"I...I don't know." *That's why I'm here*, she nearly said. After a few embarrassing questions about her menstrual history, she received the shock of her life. She was sitting down, otherwise she would have collapsed in a screaming heap on the surgery floor. Never in her worst nightmare had she expected to hear the words, *You could be pregnant*. Nothing that had happened to her before was as diabolical as this. Her hands shook so badly she had to clasp them together.

"Pregnant!" She forced herself not to start screaming. Once she started she would never be able to stop.

Don't panic, she kept telling herself as she staggered home. It could be a mistake. Deep down, she knew it wasn't. Bryce's baby grew inside her. She was going to be an unwed mother. The disgrace. She would be stigmatized when it got out. Her child would be illegitimate. Thank goodness the Sixties were a little more enlightened. A couple of generations ago, she would have been tarred and feathered before being run out of town.

Caroline rang the surgery the next day, and the test was positive. With her luck, she expected it—just what she deserved, her mother would have said.

You stupid fool, she berated herself. It took two to make a baby, but most of the responsibility rested with her. She had gone to Bryce's place knowing she diced with danger. She had encouraged, if not exactly instigated, their lovemaking. He would have stopped if she'd asked him to. He didn't need to force himself on any woman. What would he say if she told him?

He wouldn't offer love and marriage. Monetary payment, maybe, but she didn't want that from him. Better if he never knew they'd created a child together. She would resign straight away. It was imperative she find another job quickly. No way would she be hiding away in some home for unmarried mothers. She would be keeping her baby, but she needed to work out a survival plan for both of them.

On Friday she handed her resignation to Mr. Davies. "Could you make sure Mr. Harrington gets this, please?" Her hand trembled as she handed him the envelope. "It's my resignation."

"I'm sorry to be losing you." He didn't even try to talk her into staying. "A fresh start somewhere else is what you need." He sounded so concerned she could have wept.

She had sensed him staring at her on several occasions over the last few days. Did he suspect her condition? She broke out in a cold sweat.

Caroline spent a miserable weekend, half of it being sick.

"Harrington's got you pregnant," Kerry shrilled, punching the air with her fist.

"Yes, but..."

"I knew it. You've been acting strange, sort of haunted, since that Christmas breakup party. Even Trevor commented on it. You stayed the night with that bastard, didn't you?" Kerry marched up and down like some demented marionette.

"Yes." Caroline's eyes filled with tears.

"You crazy little fool. How could you?"

"I love him. Can't you understand?" Caroline gnawed at her knuckles. "It, it just happened."

"*You* might love *him*, but a rat like him would seduce you without a second thought. A man can have sex without loving a woman, you know. She only needs to be attractive enough to appeal to his male libido."

"I know, I know, but he had too much to drink. We both did. I've handed in my resignation. I'm leaving Harringtons as soon as I can."

"Have you told Andy yet?"

"No, I don't want to worry him until he gets a permanent posting. There's not much he can do, anyway. Nothing anyone can do." She blinked back the tears. If she didn't stop crying, she would end up dehydrated.

"What about Harrington? Tell him." Kerry spat the words out in an angry staccato. "He got you into this mess. Make him face up to his responsibilities."

"Please, Kerry, don't tell him," Caroline pleaded. "It wouldn't do any good. I can't blame anyone else. I threw myself at him."

She sank into the armchair and wept.

Chapter 11

On Monday Caroline got ready for work. She still didn't feel well, and a glance in the mirror confirmed her worst fears. She looked an absolute wreck. Pale skin, dark rings under her eyes. The doctor had prescribed some tablets that took away the worst of the morning sickness; otherwise she wouldn't have been able to get out of bed.

When she reached her office, she was shocked to find Bryce waiting for her. Fit and suntanned, devastatingly handsome, he lolled against her desk.

"Did you have a good holiday? You've got a nice tan." She had become a talented actress, no doubt about it.

"Yes I had a great time, but you don't look so good. Is something wrong?"

Is something wrong? she thought hysterically. Here was her chance to unburden herself, but she couldn't do it.

"No, nothing's wrong," she lied. *You just got me pregnant.* What would he say if he knew? "I've had a touch of gastro, I think, but I'm recovering now."

"Good." He grinned, showing off the dimple in his chin, and a set of even white teeth. "I'm going to keep you busy for the next few days. Geoff did a great job, but I'd like to get back into the swing of things straight away."

He gave her another devastating smile and walked back into his office. She watched him hungrily, devouring every inch of him. Straight back, broad shoulders, neat backside, long legs. The perfect specimen of powerful, virile manhood.

She pulled the cover off her typewriter and inserted some clean paper and started typing out the letters she hadn't finished on Friday.

The connecting door banged open. The room shook with the vibration. In three strides Bryce stood in front of her, his face contorted with anger. "What the hell's the meaning of this?" He threw her resignation on the desk.

"I'm resigning. I feel like a change." She couldn't look

him in the face.

"Why? Did something happen while I was away?"

Did something happen while he was away? What an understatement.

"No, I...I felt like a change."

"The hell you did. Look at me." He put a strong, tanned finger under her chin and raised her face. She watched a muscle convulse at the side of his jaw. "Why?"

"I told you."

"Don't lie to me. I know things haven't been easy lately, but you're a good secretary. We make a good team. I don't want to lose you. If it's more money, just name your price. I've been intending to give you a raise."

"It isn't more money. I just want to leave."

"If you leave, you go now. Understand? Now," he snarled. "And don't bother asking me for a reference, because you won't get it."

He crumpled her resignation into a ball and threw it in the rubbish basket, turned on his heel and stalked off.

Caroline gathered her things together and, blinking back tears, walked out of the executive office suite, leaving her heart behind. There would never be another man for her. She loved Bryce too much to ever forget him. A bitter laugh welled up in her throat. Purely academic. Few men would be prepared to accept a woman with an illegitimate baby.

Sunk in the black depths of misery, she didn't watch where she was walking and cannoned into Mr. Davies near the elevator.

"Caroline, what's wrong?"

"Mr. Harrington told me to get out if I wouldn't take back my resignation."

"There, there. Bryce doesn't mean it. He lost his temper, that's all."

"He said he wouldn't give me a reference." Her eyes swam with tears. "I have to get another job. I'm desperate. I can't be unemployed."

"Don't worry." He patted her arm. "Give my name as a reference. I'll be glad to tell any prospective employer what a gem of a secretary he's going to get."

"You've been kind. I enjoyed working for you." She smiled wistfully and walked out the door of Harrington

Constructions, never to return.

****

Bryce stormed into Geoff Davies' office. "Where's Caroline?"

"She's gone. I ran into her a couple of minutes ago."

"Did she tell you she walked out on me?" Bryce raged.

"No. She told me you wouldn't accept her resignation and asked her to withdraw it or leave."

"Damn it! She was the best secretary I ever had."

"Serves you right," Geoff said unsympathetically. "You've given that poor girl hell for months. I'm surprised she stood it this long."

"All right. I admit I'm hot-tempered and fly off the handle, but she knew that. Caroline understood me."

"Did she? You're a fool, Bryce, a blind fool. Surely you knew she was in love with you. You could see it in her eyes. You can't be that obtuse."

"I didn't notice anything. Hell, she's my secretary."

"Yes, your secretary, and I bet you let her know it, too. The girl was in love with you, and you got her to order flowers and arrange restaurant dates for your other female companions. What do you think that did to her? I'd guarantee it would have ripped her apart."

"I didn't realize. I swear it." Caroline loved him? No, it was impossible. Geoff carried on like an old woman sometimes. She had whispered "I love you" that night at his apartment, but women always said things they didn't mean in the throes of passion. But what if she really did love him? Oh, God. He thrust trembling fingers through his hair. She did stare intently at him sometimes, but he thought she was admiring his tie.

"You broke that poor girl's heart. I suppose she decided she couldn't take any more. She's looked sick for the last week or two. I sent her home one day because she fainted in the elevator."

"Sick?" Bryce asked frantically. "What do you mean, sick?"

"Probably gastric flu. It's been going around. I got a dose of it myself, very nasty. Yet, I don't know. Up close to her, you know, those huge eyes of hers seemed, well, somehow haunted."

"Imagination. Do you think she'll come back?" Bryce

lit a cigarette.

"I doubt it. She said you refused to give her a reference, so I told her I would."

"You can't. Don't you see?" Bryce drew viciously on his cigarette. "If she can't get a job anywhere else, and she won't without a reference, she'll come back to me."

"Don't bet on it. Did you have anything else you wanted to discuss?"

"No, damn it." Bryce stalked out of the room.

****

It took Caroline a week to find a suitable position as secretary in a lawyer's office. Her elderly boss hadn't been happy about employing someone as young as she was, but the glowing reference from Geoff Davies had convinced him to at least give her a try.

What a dull job, typing up wills, affidavits and various other dry legal documents. Pity he wasn't a criminal lawyer. Then she would have been typing up heaps of interesting cases. Another part of her job entailed going to the Registrar of Land Titles, searching out titles for clients buying real estate. This was her favorite duty, as it got her out of the office and into the fresh air for a time.

About three weeks after she left Harringtons, a check for five hundred dollars arrived in the mail. It had been signed by Bryce.

"The golden handshake for services rendered," she commented bitterly to Kerry. "I feel like tearing it up."

"Don't be stupid," her friend remonstrated with her. "You'll need every cent you can get your hands on. You won't be able to work forever, you know, and what about after the baby is born?"

"I'll cope. Others have done it. Once Andy gets a permanent posting, he'll help me." Caroline tried to sound confident. In reality, she was terrified.

"You won't consider adoption, I suppose?"

"Never." Not her baby, Bryce's baby. She would fight to the death to protect it. She'd sell herself in the street if necessary.

****

Andy met Kerry in a cafe near the Flinders Street railway station and they shared some sandwiches.

"Tell me, now, what's wrong?" He took his cap off and rubbed the back of his hand across his forehead. "I haven't had a minute's peace since you rang me."

"I don't know of any other way to tell you this, so I'll be blunt. Caroline is pregnant."

"What!" His loud exclamation caused several heads to swivel in their direction.

Kerry told him the whole story.

"Rotten bastard! I ought to kill him!"

"Keep your voice down, or you'll get us arrested. Caroline didn't want to tell you yet, but I had to do something. She's got me worried. I wanted her to front Harrington, even volunteered to go with her or see him myself, but she refused. Begged me to keep away from him."

"I'll see him. Where's that office again?" Andy pushed his sandwiches to one side.

"You might as well finish your lunch first." Kerry smiled at him to lighten the moment.

"I'll choke if I eat them. I'd like to ram them down Harrington's throat."

"I have to get back to work now. My boss, miserable old goat, wasn't too happy about giving me the time off. Let me know what happens, won't you?"

"Yes, I will. Thanks for telling me. I appreciate it."

Andy arrived at the Harrington building just before three o'clock and asked at reception for the correct floor. Standing in the elevator, he clenched his hands into fists. How could a man do this to his softhearted, gullible sister? His hate and fury climbed to boiling point. It took all his army training to keep it under control.

As the elevator door opened he charged out and marched to where he could hear typewriters clacking. He poked his head around the door of the typing pool, then strode over to the middle-aged woman who seemed to be in charge. So, this was Miss Bumpstead, the old battleaxe Caroline had mentioned. Typical old maid, hard-faced, sour.

"I want to see Bryce Harrington. Where's his office, please?" He didn't know where he dredged the strength from to speak civilly.

"Mr. Harrington never sees people without an

appointment," Miss Bumpstead replied primly.

"Where's his office? I'm not leaving until you tell me." Grudgingly, she told him.

He found Caroline's office without much trouble. A woman of about forty sat at the desk, typing.

"I want to see Bryce Harrington."

"I'm sorry. Mr. Harrington is holding an important meeting in his office and can't be disturbed. I'll make an appointment for you to see him later on."

"To hell with his meeting. That's his door, isn't it?" Andy strode across the room, snatching off his cap as he did so.

"You can't go in there."

"Yeah? Try stopping me."

Without knocking, he flung the door open and started across the room. So, this was the inner sanctum.

"Harrington, I want to speak to you."

Five sets of eyes swiveled towards him.

"What the hell are you doing, bursting into my office like this? I told my secretary I wasn't to be disturbed."

"Too bad. I've got something to say to you. Frankly, I don't give a damn whether I say it in public or private."

He watched Harrington get to his feet and take up a threatening stance. "I'm asking you to leave, or I'll have you thrown out by security."

"I'm not leaving. I've traveled over a hundred miles to get here, and neither you nor any of your paid henchmen can stop me saying my piece. It's about Caroline and the firm's Christmas party."

Andy noticed with satisfaction how a slight flush crept up Harrington's cheeks.

"Go and have a coffee break. We'll recommence the meeting in fifteen minutes or so."

"What I've got to say won't take fifteen minutes—more like five. I couldn't stand being in the same room with you for any longer, Harrington."

There was a shocked silence.

"Fifteen minutes," Bryce snapped the words out, and the other men left. He lit a cigarette and inhaled deeply.

"What do you want—Andy, isn't it?"

"I've come because of what you did to Caroline."

"Jealous, soldier boy, that she preferred me to you?"

"You filthy bastard! I ought to kill you! Caroline's my sister."

"I'm sorry. I shouldn't have made that remark anyway."

"No, you shouldn't have. There are lots of things you shouldn't have done." Andy spat the words out. "You seduced my sister, got her pregnant, then fired her."

"What did you say?"

"You heard me the first time," Andy retorted furiously, "but I'll repeat it. You seduced my sister, got her pregnant, and then fired her."

"Pregnant!" Harrington looked as if he'd been knifed in the guts. "What the hell are you raving about?"

"Yeah, pregnant, and I want to know what you're going to do about it? You're not getting my sister into trouble and leaving her to struggle on alone."

"Sit down. For God's sake! I didn't know she was pregnant. I never gave it a thought."

"No, I'll bet you didn't," Andy replied scathingly.

"Did Caroline ask you to come and see me?"

"No. She hasn't even told me. Kerry rang me up at the base. She's worried sick. I haven't seen Caroline since Christmas." He thumped the desk with a clenched fist.

Bryce glared at him. "For God's sake, can't you be reasonable about this? How did an immature, hot-headed kid like you get selected for officer training?"

"The old school tie, dear boy. If you go to the right school, anything's possible. If your father was a decorated officer it helps, also, but we're digressing. I came to see you about Caroline, not to discuss my military career."

"All right. I give you my word I'll go and see her. We'll work something out."

"How can I trust your word after what you did?" Andy retorted.

"For God's sake, I'm not proud of what happened, and naturally I'll make myself responsible for her expenses."

"Big of you, I'm sure. If you think you can wipe the slate clean by paying her to dump the kid off at some orphanage, forget it. Kerry said Caroline is adamant, she wants to keep it."

"Young fool. I'll go and see her."

"You'd like that, wouldn't you? Persuade her to get

rid of the kid, and you're off the hook."

"Don't be ridiculous," Bryce snarled. "Give me a chance to think this through. I'll go and see her tonight. We can discuss everything civilly and work out what's best to do."

"How can I trust you?"

Andy watched Bryce's face darken in temper. "I've given you my word. I'll see her tonight."

"I have to get back to camp. You'd better work something out, because I'm warning you I'll drag your name through the gutter press if I have to. I won't stand by and let my sister be hurt any more." Andy strode towards the door and wrenched it open.

"Just a minute," Bryce called him back. "What school did you go to?"

"Melbourne Grammar," Andy flung the words over his shoulder. "If it's any of your business."

"That's the school I went to. You just about have to be the son of an old boy to get in."

"I know." Who the hell did Harrington think he was? Bloody snob. "I am the son of an old boy. My father and grandfather both attended there. Caroline went to the girl's college. I have to get back to base. Can't say it's been a pleasure." Andy slammed the door behind him, hoping it would fall off its hinges.

****

Bryce sat at his desk feeling as if he had just been gutted. Andy's words explained a lot of things about Caroline. The way she spoke, the swimming coach, even the way she walked. No wonder his father knew the name. He must have gone to school with their father. I've got her pregnant. He held his head in his hands. How the hell was he going to sit through this bloody meeting? His father would be mortified. Thank God he wasn't here. *Only decent break I've had all day.*

Caroline pregnant. He'd never given a thought to such a thing. No wonder she'd been sick—that explained her hurried departure.

What an idiot. He slammed his fist on the desk. One night. One bloody night. He'd always left the matter of contraception up to the women, and all the ones he associated with knew how to take care of themselves. He

Cardinal Sin

hadn't known Caroline was a virgin. He tried to excuse himself, but he was honest enough to admit that, fueled by alcohol, he'd wanted her so badly he wouldn't have given it a second thought. What a mess. He groaned out loud.

The men returned. "Who was that?" Geoff Davies asked.

"Caroline's brother."

"I didn't know she had a brother."

"I knew she had a brother," Bryce replied savagely, "but I didn't know he was a hotheaded, pretty-looking soldier boy."

"What did he want?"

"It's a private matter," Bryce snapped.

He knew Geoff was curious, but no way would he be satisfying the older man's curiosity. The fewer people who knew about this debacle the better.

With an effort, he pulled himself together and carried on with the meeting. Sheer willpower kept him glued to his chair when he felt like going to the nearest bar and getting blind rotten drunk. As soon as the meeting finished, he vowed to himself, he'd go over to his club for a few drinks while he worked out the best course of action.

Chapter 12

It was nearly six o'clock by the time Bryce arrived at his club. He couldn't get a parking spot and had to park out in the street. How come every other club member had decided to come here tonight, he fumed. It was a dead-set certainty no one else's need was as great as his.

He stalked into the club lounge. Might as well have dinner here, too, although he felt sure he couldn't eat a bite.

He met up with a couple of business acquaintances who were dining here, also. Their wives were at some hen meeting, seafood and champagne dinner to follow. Typical. Just the kind of social affair that appealed to his mother.

He couldn't stop thinking about Caroline. What would he say to her? This was one confrontation he dreaded. Morosely he chewed on a piece of veal steak. It had been marinated in wine, but for all the enjoyment he got out of it, he might as well have ordered stale bread.

He answered his companions in a distracted manner. They kept looking at him strangely, but he didn't care as he gulped down a couple of glasses of wine. Alcohol wasn't going to help. It had gotten him into this terrible mess.

"You okay, Bryce?" one of his companions asked.

"Yes. Of course I'm all right." It took all his control to answer without snarling. "I've just had a trying day." What an understatement. It had been a real shocker. "I've got an appointment." He glanced at his watch. "See you later."

Striding out of the club, he wished he hadn't bothered to call in. The whole situation was a bloody mess.

He drove to Caroline's apartment and parked outside in the street, making sure all his doors were locked. That would be the last straw, if some deadbeat stole his car.

His knock on the door was answered by Kerry, who eyed him with dislike.

"Is Caroline here?"

"What if she is?"

"Because I want to see her, damn you."

"Well, she mightn't want to see you, you arrogant, egotistical brute. Did you ever think of that? She's learnt the hard way what kind of man you are."

"Meaning what?" He pushed past Kerry and strode into the sitting room.

"Where is she?"

"She's lying down. She gets tired easily these days."

"I've got the message. Her brother gave it to me loud and clear," he ground out as he strode into the bedroom.

The blinds had been drawn, plunging the room into semi-darkness, but that didn't do much to hide the shabbiness. Caroline lay on the bed in her bra and panties. Her head was turned away from him, so he didn't know whether she was asleep or not.

He couldn't stop himself from staring at her white breasts as they peeped out over her lacy bra. His scrutiny continued. Her stomach looked smooth and flat. Maybe she wasn't pregnant, after all. The oldest trick in the book. How many men had been trapped that way over the years? What on earth was he thinking about? He shook himself mentally. She'd hardly be two months gone.

What he knew about pregnancy would fit on a postage stamp, but even he knew she wouldn't be showing yet. Besides, that was no act her brother had put on. He'd stormed into the office with murder in his eye.

He moved towards the bed and hovered there. Maybe she was asleep. Perhaps he shouldn't wake her. But that was only an excuse, and he knew it, to delay the matter. *What am I, a man or a mouse?*

"Caroline." He hadn't meant to use that tone. It just came out that way.

She turned her head, and he watched bemusement in her eyes give way to shock. She had obviously been asleep.

"What do you want?" Her voice came out in a throaty whisper.

"I want to talk to you. Er, could you put some clothes on?" He couldn't stop staring at her almost naked body—it mesmerized him.

"Where's my brunch coat?" She glanced around.

"This do?" He reached out and flicked a cotton dressing gown off the door handle and gave it to her.

"I don't think we've got anything to talk about. I won't come back to work for you."

"You know damn well I haven't come to talk about that. I got a visit from your big brother, the army captain, uniform and all," he went on sarcastically. "I thought he was going to challenge me to meet him at daybreak with pistols drawn."

"What do you mean?" Her voice was low, and he sensed she fought back tears. At any other time he would have felt sorry for her, but the only sorry feeling he had at the moment was for himself.

"Why the hell didn't you tell me you were pregnant? Up and leaving like that. What kind of man do you think I am?"

"Not much of a one," Kerry said, as she entered the room.

"Get out. This is a private conversation."

"You happen to be sitting on my bed."

Caroline started crying.

"You've upset her, you callous beast. Leave before I call the police," Kerry attacked him.

"You listen to me. I've taken enough abuse for one day. I've come over prepared to be reasonable and sort out this mess." It sounded pompous and he knew it. He clenched his fist in his pocket. "I haven't got all night. I want to get everything cleared up now."

"Another date? The full seduction routine, I suppose," Kerry jeered.

"Get out. I'm warning you, or so help me..." His hand fisted in his pocket.

"Could I offer you coffee, laced with arsenic, of course?" she said as a parting shot.

The breath hissed from between his clenched teeth. "Why didn't you tell me, Caroline, for God's sake?"

"Why should I? You didn't care about me after you got what you wanted," she answered bitterly.

That shook him. He'd never known her to be bitter before.

"I want to help."

"Do you? Really? It's a wonder you don't accuse me of lying about being pregnant and trying to put the blame on you."

"I admit the responsibility is mine, and I'm prepared to help. I've just said that."

"Think you'll buy me off, do you? A few hundred dollars to pay for an abortion, and your conscience will be clear."

"Abortion!" That shocked him. He didn't like the thought one little bit.

"What's it to you?"

"Don't be bitter." He put his finger under her chin and lifted her face up so he could stare straight into her eyes.

"Do you want an abortion? Honestly, do you?" He watched her eyes fill with tears.

"No, I'm not having an abortion. It's my baby, and I'm keeping it."

He wondered why that pleased him. Then he felt as if she had kicked him in the stomach when she went on, passionately.

"I'll sell myself in the street, if I have to. I'll do anything to keep my baby. You hear me? Anything! Now please go away and leave me alone." She started crying again.

"Don't upset yourself." God, he needed a drink—several drinks, in fact. "I'm prepared to help you. Give up your job. I'll pay you an allowance and be responsible for all your expenses."

"Don't bother. I don't want your charity."

He ground his teeth. "It's not charity."

"What would you call it? Your Christian duty? Conscience money? Tell me, Bryce, what would you call it?"

"I'm going." He ground the words out. "I'll come back when you're prepared to listen to reason." He strode out of the apartment, slamming the door behind him. Those two girls would drive him into the lunatic asylum in next to no time.

Caroline was upset. Hadn't he read somewhere how easily pregnant women got upset, hormonal changes or some such rubbish? He'd leave it for a day or two before coming to see her again. *I'll buy her a house, something with a garden.* Yes, she'd like that. He'd make her a generous allowance, and one for the child, also, he mused as he drove along.

The thought popped into his head that he'd like it to be a boy. He cursed under his breath. What in the name of hell was he thinking of? Why should he care? He wouldn't be having anything to do with either of them. Everything would be arranged through his lawyer. It was the only sensible course of action. He couldn't explain the vague feeling of disquiet he felt at this thought. His nerves were shot to pieces. It had been one hell of a shock.

He drew savagely on his cigarette, wondering whether he should call in and see his father, who had taken another slight heart turn the other day. This would have to be the most traumatic day of his life. Maybe he should stop and see the old boy. He was fond of his father. His mother he wasn't so sure of, though.

He should have some affection for her—she was his mother, after all. Not that he could remember her ever being maternal. A nanny had brought him up until he went to school, and servants minded him once he started school.

He could remember not seeing his mother for two or three days on end sometimes, if she got caught up with her committees or social gatherings. His father had been busy expanding the business, but the old man always made the effort to spend part of each day with him, even if it was only a quick bedtime story when he was working to a deadline.

He recalled one particular birthday when he turned seven. His mother bought him a new bicycle. She hadn't even bothered to find out if he could ride it or not. The old man taught him how to ride, watched and applauded as he gained expertise. He couldn't remember his mother ever even seeing him on it.

He slowed down at the gates, and they opened automatically for him. As usual, he admired his parents' house. Ridiculous having such a large place for just the two of them. Of course, it would be his in due course, but for a bachelor pad it was laughable.

Pulling up outside the house, he made his way to the

Cardinal Sin

verandah and banged the brass knocker rather than use his own keys. The housekeeper opened the door, all smiles.

"Good evening, Mr. Harrington."

"Good evening. Nice to see you again, Mrs. Ferguson. How's my father?" He followed her inside.

"He's not too bad. He's taking coffee in the drawing room."

"Good." He went into the drawing room, where his father reclined in his favorite Louis XV armchair.

"How are you?" He smiled at his father, untypically dressed in pajamas and matching brown dressing gown. "Where's mother?" He glanced around.

"She's on the phone, but she'll be back in a minute."

"You're looking pale. Why don't you and mother take a holiday? Get away from it all. Brampton Island would be nice, if you don't feel up to traveling overseas."

"Oh, Bryce, darling." His mother swept in. "I hope you haven't been upsetting your father with business problems. No stress, complete rest, that's what the doctor ordered. Of course, he's worried about you."

"Me! Why?"

"Your father is anxious about what's going to happen to the company, this house, everything. If only you'd be reasonable and get married, produce the grandchild he's been longing for, I'm sure everything would be all right."

"For God's sake, don't start harping on that again—I couldn't stand it. That's not worrying you, is it, Dad? I've told you before, I'll marry eventually and present you with an heir."

God, it struck him like a bolt of lightning. He wasn't married, but the heir was already on his way. Why hadn't he thought of that before? Shock must have caused a mental block.

"It would ease my mind. I don't like to push you." His father's voice trailed off wistfully.

"Yes, darling, you must do something. Ashley is such an adorable girl, or even Amanda is suitable. Her parents hoped for a match. Very embarrassing for me when I found out you'd broken off with her."

Bryce ground his teeth. They would be worn to the gums if he went through much more today. "She's a selfish, demanding bimbo," he said savagely, "and Ashley's an empty-headed one."

He clamped his teeth together as he watched his father's face pale. Scenes were no good for him. "I don't wish to discuss it, do you understand? I'll choose my own wife when I'm ready and the time is right." What an idiotic thing to say. He wasn't ready, but the time was more than right.

Caroline claimed to love him once, maybe she still did. He'd ask her to marry him. All his problems would be solved at once. He laughed, and his mother jumped on him straight away.

"What's so funny? You've a weird sense of humor. Your father is worrying himself into an early grave because you're too selfish to give him the one thing he craves." Her voice rose until it became shrill.

"All right. I'll get married. I'll produce an heir. Will that satisfy you?"

"Yes, yes." His mother sounded ecstatic. "Amanda or Ashley?"

"Neither."

"Who?"

"I know who I'm going to ask. I just have to get her to accept, that's all."

"Who is it?" his mother demanded. "Why wouldn't she accept you? You've been nominated for Bachelor of the Year several times. You're an excellent catch. How dare any woman think she's too superior to marry a Harrington?"

"You'll stop worrying, Dad, if I get married and produce an heir, right?"

"Yes, it would be a load off my mind."

"I'll be married and give you a grandchild before the end of the year. Satisfied?"

"Don't be so flippant. This is a serious matter," his mother put in.

"Don't you think I know that? Damn it all, I've agreed to do what you want, so let the matter drop. Have you got a whiskey?" he asked his father. "I need it. You should have a small one, too. I've got something I want to tell you. We'd better discuss it in the study."

"Now, look here. Your father isn't to be upset. I don't

want you burdening him with business problems."

"I know what I'm doing. Please don't interfere."

He watched his father slowly lever himself out of the chair, wondering whether he should offer to give him a hand. The old boy was fiercely independent and wouldn't thank him for treating him like an invalid.

"You all right, Dad?"

"Yes, I've just got to take it easy."

They made their way to the study. Bryce saw his father into his favorite armchair before going to the drinks cupboard and pouring out their whiskeys. He handed his father a glass. "Are you allowed to drink?"

"No, but a small one won't hurt."

"Look." Bryce cleared his throat. "I don't know whether I should be telling you this or not. Part of it will come as a shock, and some of it will be one of your dreams come true." He grinned ruefully. "You remember Caroline Dennison?"

"The girl who was your secretary? Up and left you in the lurch, didn't she? Jolly shame. I liked her."

"Remember when you said the surname rang a bell, but you couldn't think from where?"

"Yes, yes." His father was intrigued now.

"How about from school?" Did you go to school with a Dennison?"

"Dennison... yes!" He slapped the arm of his chair. "Drew Dennison joined the army. We all did. Second World War, you know, but he got killed a couple of days before the armistice. Tragic, because his brother Eddie was shot down over Germany in 1941."

"Well, Caroline's got a brother Andy—short for Andrew, I presume." Bryce's lips curled in remembrance. "Hot-headed young fool."

"Drew's name was Andrew."

"Well, this Andy has just graduated from the Military Academy. He went to Melbourne Grammar, years behind me, though. Caroline attended the girl's college."

"Ah, so that's it. I thought there seemed something familiar about her. She's got her father's eyes. I remember those big blue eyes now. He could get away with murder. Just stared at the teachers all innocent-like and got off, while the rest of us copped a caning."

"This is the part I don't know whether I should be telling you. I'm going to ask Caroline to marry me."

"What's wrong with that?" His father sounded amazed he should even ask.

"You don't mind? Mother will be furious she doesn't belong to the right social set."

"Rubbish, *you're* marrying the girl, not your mother. So, you've fallen in love at last, son."

"I didn't say that."

"You didn't? But you just said you're going to marry her."

"I am. That is, I'm going to ask her. Whether she accepts or not is a different matter. When she resigned from work she gave me some flimsy excuse about wanting a change, or some such rubbish. I spoke to her last night."

"You missed her and realized you wanted to marry her." His father beamed.

Bryce lit a cigarette. "Not exactly. Today, right in the middle of our department heads' conference, the door flies open and I'm confronted by an enraged young army captain. He called me a bastard. I've never seen anything like it. I half expected him to challenge me to a duel, pistols at fifty paces."

"Why? Did he go berserk? Some army lads suffer mental problems. Can't take the discipline. Of course, if he's been to Vietnam, he might be suffering battle fatigue."

"It's nothing like that. He was spitting fury because he said I dishonored his sister."

"You what?" Alexander went to stand up.

"Don't get up. He told me, well, he said I got her pregnant."

"You what? Did you deny it? Threaten to sue?" Alexander thumped his fist on the arm of his chair.

"How could I sue him? It was the truth. I did get her pregnant."

"You shouldn't joke about things like that. It isn't decent."

"I'm telling you." Bryce thrust his fingers through his hair. "I got Caroline pregnant. Remember the night of the staff Christmas party, when I took her home? Well, we went to my apartment and she stayed the night."

Cardinal Sin

"That doesn't mean anything. Young women these days are in and out of bed at the drop of a hat. Free love they call it, I think. She didn't look the hippie type."

There was a bluish tinge to his father's lips and Bryce wondered whether he was doing the right thing. Too late now. He was in so deep he couldn't do anything except press on.

"She's not the type. I'm not a complete fool. I'd had a fair bit to drink, but I wasn't too drunk to know she hadn't been with a man before."

"You seduced her, when you knew?" His father looked mortified.

"No, of course I didn't. I wouldn't have taken her to my apartment if I'd known. God, what do you take me for? By the time I realized, well, it was too late."

"My boy, I don't know what to say."

"She was in love with me, and I got her a bit tipsy. That's why she left work. Didn't want me to know. Didn't even tell her brother. Her crazy shrew of a friend told him, and he came charging in ready to fight me to the death. She never even bloody told me," he said savagely. "I had a right to know. It's my child, too, isn't it?" He completely disregarded the fact he hadn't wanted anything to do with it earlier in the day. "I saw her before coming here, as a matter of fact."

"You offered to marry her?"

"No. I didn't want to get married, you know that. I told her I'd be responsible for her expenses and give her an allowance, that type of thing. She called it conscience money. Said she didn't need my charity. As for that freaky friend of hers, she hates my guts and doesn't bother to hide it." He clenched his fist. Each time he thought of the shrewish Kerry he felt murderous.

"Well, I don't blame the girl. You can see her side of it."

"Why? What about my side of it? I did the right thing. I offered to take care of everything," he answered self-righteously. God, what was wrong with him?

"Now you've suddenly decided you want to marry her," his father put in astutely.

"No, well, yes. You've got your heart set on an heir, and there's one on the way. It would be the best solution all round."

"You said you didn't love the girl," Alexander put in. Bryce started to think his father was enjoying his discomfort.

"So what? I don't think I'm in love." He threw his hands in the air. "How do I know? I've never been in love before. Let's face it. I'd rather have her for a wife than some of those scheming bimbos Mother keeps lining up for me. There's no guarantee they would or could give me a child, but this way it's a certainty." The more he thought about the idea, the more he liked it.

"What will you tell your mother?"

"The truth, I suppose. I thought I might let you break the news to her." Bryce grinned for the first time in hours. "She won't carry on so much if you tell her. I'll go and see Caroline tomorrow. If she's agreeable, I'll contact Russ. Remember Russell Stevenson? I went to school with him. He's the school chaplain now. He'd marry us without any fuss or bother. That's another thing—I don't want Mother interfering. I want to get married as quickly and painlessly as possible. All I've got to do is persuade Caroline."

"Well, you did treat her rather shabbily. It will serve you right if she turns you down flat. The fact that she's pregnant ought to help you, though, I guess. There again, pregnant women can be quite unpredictable."

Bryce grimaced. "I'll have another whiskey." He went over and filled his glass. "You're not too upset?"

"Upset? No, I'm pleased. My only worry is that she might turn you down. I think she'll make an ideal wife. When did you say the baby was due?" He rubbed his hands together in what looked a gleeful manner.

At least someone's happy, Bryce thought bitterly. The old man would probably be the only one. The whole situation was a mess.

"How would I know when it's due? I didn't even try to work it out. I've had a hell of a day. I've got too much on my mind to worry about crap like that." He could feel the anger welling up inside him again. It was a miracle he hadn't had a nervous breakdown.

"Well, everyone else will, you can be sure of it. Nothing they'd like better." Alexander chuckled.

"It's not a laughing matter. Not that it worries me, but Mother won't like it." If things weren't so drastic it would be almost funny. He could just picture his mother trying to invent some excuse to her friends over their morning cocktails.

His father must have thought along similar lines, because he burst out laughing. "She'll have to tell everyone it's premature. Too bad if it's a ten-pound baby." Alexander laughed again. He suddenly looked twenty years younger.

Bryce stared at his father, hoping his mouth wasn't hanging open.

"I'm off. I'll see Mother on the way out."

"I'll come with you. Pity you can't be here when I break the news." He laughed again. Surely his father wasn't drunk. He'd only had half a glass of whiskey.

They walked back to the sitting room, where his mother waited. It wasn't a laughing matter. Marriage didn't appeal to him one little bit. He'd probably be a lousy husband, and as for what kind of father he would make, it just didn't bear thinking about. How the old man could be so cheerful was a mystery. The whole situation was a bloody nightmare.

"Well, you're certainly cheerful, Alexander. Has Bryce made you another million or two?"

"No, no, better than another million. I'm going to be a grandfather." He positively beamed.

Bryce, watching his mother, saw her lips compress, and he wished his father had waited until he'd gone before saying anything.

"What are you raving about? You weren't in that study drinking, were you?"

"No, dear." Alexander laughed again. "Bryce is going to become a father in, um, about September. See, I worked it out."

His mother was struck speechless for a moment. "You are joking, naturally." Her voice became frigid.

"I'm quite serious. This is the best news I've heard in years."

"I'm off. I'll leave you to explain everything. Good night." And with that, Bryce scurried out of the room like a rat leaving the proverbial sinking ship.

"Come back! What is going on? I demand to know."

He ignored his mother and kept on going. *I won't forget this day in a hurry*, he thought as he climbed into his car and slammed the door.

Chapter 13

After Bryce left the apartment, Kerry came into the bedroom with a cup of tea for Caroline. "You shouldn't have told Andy. You promised."

"I had to tell him. I've been worried sick about you. I couldn't have it on my conscience. Boy, I wish I'd been a fly on the wall when Andy burst into Harrington's office. Bet he gave Mr. High-and-Mighty the shock of his life. I shouldn't have been eavesdropping while he was here, but I couldn't help it."

"He offered me money. Did you hear that?"

"No, I didn't listen all the time, but why shouldn't he support you? It's his fault you're in this mess."

"I turned him down. No way am I going to accept his grudging charity," Caroline said bitterly. "He thought he could pay me off."

"You're mad."

"I couldn't help it. I love him. I should hate him for what he's done, but I can't. I'm not taking money from him. I'd rather starve. He said he would come back and discuss things again when I became more reasonable. He expects me to be reasonable." Caroline snapped a biscuit between her teeth.

"You're priceless, you know that? We'll have to ring Andy. I'll bet he's dying to know what happened," Kerry went on. "Gee, was he mad."

"He'll worry now. I wish you hadn't."

"He had a right to know. He's your only relative. Actually, he got upset because you didn't confide in him."

Caroline dragged herself out of bed for work the next morning. She had been crying half the night and looked it. Her face was pale and blotchy, and she had bags under her eyes. Bryce didn't love her. Andy was upset about her predicament. And if she could believe the papers, he would soon be on his way to Vietnam. No wonder she couldn't stop crying long enough to get some sleep.

She listlessly pushed the toast around on her plate but drank the tea Kerry had made for her.

"Eat up." Kerry stood over her like a general. "You're not leaving here until you do."

She forced the toast into her mouth, wondering why she didn't gag on every mouthful. Don't think. Just chew and swallow. It was imperative that she snap out of her malaise, and she would. Surely she was entitled to a few days of self pity, though. Plenty of time to be strong and brave. Once she felt her baby's movements her strength and determination would return. She could take on the world and win.

She pulled herself together enough to pick up her handbag and walk down to the bus stop with Kerry. As always, the bus was full, but by pushing and shoving Kerry got her a seat. A ruddy-faced business man carrying a black briefcase gave them both a hostile stare.

"Who does he think he is?" Kerry hissed in Caroline's ear. "Chauvinist pig."

****

Caroline unlocked the door of her office. Now that her boss trusted her, she opened the office so he could see clients on his way to work. She put her bag on the desk, lifted the cover off her typewriter and got busy.

Mr. Jackson, a short pompous man who always wore a charcoal gray suit and a blue shirt, arrived a little after ten. He mopped his brow with a white handkerchief. He hated the heat but was too conservative to discard his suit and tie for something cooler.

"So, this is where you're working." Caroline nearly collapsed as Bryce strode into her office.

"What are you doing here?" she asked belligerently, even though her heart leapt at the sight of him.

"I've come to see you, not to make my last will and testament. That dumpy little guy who just came in, is he your boss?"

"Yes."

"Good. Tell him you want the morning off."

"I don't want the morning off."

"You might not want it off, but you're having it. Give him your resignation at the same time. Tell him to his face, though. Don't leave a crappy little note on his desk like you did to me."

"You've got no right. I don't work for you now."

"I've got every right. Go and tell him, or I will, and believe me, I'm not in the mood for sweet talk, either."

Mr. Jackson came out just then. "Miss Dennison..." He stopped, his face registering surprise when he noticed Bryce. "Could I help you?"

"Caroline, er, Miss Dennison would like the morning off."

"I beg your pardon?"

"You heard me," Bryce said curtly. "Miss Dennison requires the morning off. She also wishes to hand in her resignation as from now, but she can work until Tuesday or Wednesday to give you a chance to find a replacement."

"What gives you the authority to interfere?" Mr. Jackson blustered.

"The fact that she is going to be my wife in just over a week gives me all the right in the world."

Caroline couldn't believe she was hearing right. She stared at Bryce, too stunned to move.

"Grab your bag, for heaven's sake." He picked up her bag and, with his hand clamped around her elbow, marched her to the door. "She'll be back after lunch," he threw the words over his shoulder.

"H...Have you gone m...mad?"

"Mad? No, I'm quite sane. We're getting married in a week. You've got to fill in some papers, and I've got to buy you a wedding ring."

"You are mad. I'm not marrying you."

"Oh, but you are," he answered with arrogant confidence.

"Since when?"

"Last night, when I worked out that this is the only sensible course of action for us."

"I don't have to marry you if I don't want to." If he loved her she would be the happiest girl in the world.

"Yes, you do. I've already notified your brother. He'll be there to give you away on Saturday. We're being married at five o'clock in the Melbourne Grammar chapel. The minister happens to be a friend of mine. It's all arranged," he said smugly.

"I haven't agreed to marry you."

"Haven't you, honey? But you will. I'm supposed to be an excellent catch."

"I don't know." She gnawed her lip. "It's because of the baby, isn't it?"

"Yes. I'm not giving up my bachelor lifestyle without good reason. I want my child to carry my name. Your brother called me a bastard, and I don't want any child of mine being called that."

"It couldn't work. A shotgun marriage would be doomed before it even started." Her eyes filled with tears.

He put his arm around her and pulled her close. His warm breath caressed her cheek. She felt an overwhelming desire to rest her cheek against his chest. To hear his heart beat. Inhale his male scent.

"It's the only sensible thing to do. We'll see the minister and sign the papers, and I'll organize a wedding ring. We'll have some lunch, and then I'll take you back to work, so your boss won't blow a gasket."

When they came to the car, he opened the door to let her in, then went around to the driver's side. Before he drove away, he lit a cigarette.

Caroline's mind was in turmoil. Bryce wanted to marry her. She loved him desperately and should have been happy, but he didn't love her. He just wanted to do the decent thing and give their child his name.

She should have jumped out of the Jaguar, but she didn't. Should have refused to sign the papers at the church or accept the minister's congratulations, but she didn't. Did she have no pride at all? Not when it came to Bryce Harrington. She was putty in his hands, easily moulded to his will.

They went to an exclusive jewelry store, where she chose a plain gold wedding ring.

"I'll buy you an engagement ring later on. There's some antique family stuff in the safe at home. You can have a look at it. There are a couple of rings you might fancy. If not, I'll have one made for you."

They ate lunch at a small, exclusive restaurant, roast duckling, cooked to perfection, but she couldn't do it justice.

"Would you care for dessert?" he asked.

"No, thanks."

Cardinal Sin

"You've lost weight, and you're pecking at your food like a bird. I remember when we went out you ate quite heartily. Have some dessert, go on," he wheedled.

"I don't want any. I'll be sick. Rich food makes me nauseous."

"I keep forgetting." He frowned. "Have you seen a doctor?"

"Yes. He prescribed some tablets for the nausea."

"Well, what's your problem, then? How about a coffee?"

"Could I have tea? I can't drink coffee, either." She thought she heard him curse, but he ordered tea for her, coffee for himself.

"What's the point of taking bloody tablets if they don't work?"

"They stop the morning sickness, but certain foods still don't agree with me anymore."

"I give up." He held his head in his hands. "Women."

"It isn't my fault." She hated sounding whiney and tearful all the time.

"All right." He patted her arm. "I'm sorry. I just don't understand any of this. I know nothing about pregnancy."

"I don't know much, either."

"Don't worry, there must be classes or something we can take, to learn the ropes."

She realized he was trying to be helpful, but every word he uttered made her feel even more incompetent.

"I'm going to be busy over the next few days, so we probably won't see each other until we meet at the chapel."

Their coffee and tea arrived. She drank hers slowly, while he sculled his in a couple of mouthfuls. She wondered why it didn't scald him.

"It was half cold." He might have read her mind. "I felt it the moment I picked the cup up. Don't get all huffy on me, but I've opened a couple of accounts for you."

He leaned across and put his finger against her lips to stall her argument. "You're to spend Thursday and Friday shopping. Buy a complete wardrobe, you understand. Everything. If you don't buy what I want, I'll come with you and buy it myself. Understood?"

"Yes."

"Good, we won't be going on a honeymoon." She watched his lips curl. "I've already had my holidays."

What about me? she nearly said. *I've worked like a galley slave without a break for months.*

"For the time being, we'll live in my apartment. We'll think about getting another place later on. Pack what you want to bring with you, and I'll send someone over on Friday to collect it. That's all. I think I've covered everything."

Yes, he'd thought of everything in his usual, analytic way. She was mad to be marrying him, but she loved him so much she would take him on any terms. Besides, regardless of her proclamation to Kerry, she wasn't brave enough to bring up a baby on her own.

She returned to work, where a frigid reception awaited her. Later in the afternoon a large city employment agency sent over a middle-aged woman who seemed perfect for the job. Mr. Jackson acted more reasonable after that.

When Caroline arrived home, she told Kerry what had happened.

"It's the least he can do. Mr. High-and-Mighty owes you—big time."

"Will you and Trevor come to the wedding? I know you don't like Bryce, but I'd like to have you there."

"Sure, we'll come. It's the least we can do for a pal. You'll need plenty of moral support. I wonder what your future in-laws are like?"

"Mr. Harrington is a nice man. I haven't met his wife, but from all accounts she's a first-rate snob. Bryce doesn't mention her much. I get the impression they aren't close."

Andy would be coming down on Saturday morning, according to Bryce. He wasn't due for a leave pass, but Harrington Senior, who knew someone high up in the army, had pulled strings.

Money opens lots of doors, Caroline thought cynically. Could it save her brother from the killing fields of Vietnam?

On Thursday, Kerry took the day off work and they went on a shopping spree. Caroline bought a whole wardrobe of new clothes. She spent large sums of money in an exclusive boutique. Kerry made sure she did. It was rather fun not having to worry about blowing your budget.

Frothy nightgowns, silky underwear, dresses, slack suits, new bathers and several after-five frocks. They spent Bryce's money with reckless abandonment.

"Serves him right," Kerry said when Caroline protested. "He owes you this and more. Wonder what Amanda and the other bimbos will have to say about him marrying you? Bet they'll be as jealous as hell."

"It's not funny. They'll hate me. All the women coveted Bryce. I suppose they'll still chase after him, whether he's married or not."

"Don't worry, Caro. You got him to the altar. That's more than any of them could do."

"The bimbos didn't let themselves get pregnant, and they aren't having a shotgun wedding."

"Yeah, but I bet they wish they were. I've got a good mind to ring up the newspapers, so you can have your picture in the social columns."

"No, please! If you contact the papers, I'll never speak to you again. Never, you understand?"

"Only kidding." Kerry laughed as she squeezed Caroline's hand.

For her wedding outfit Caroline chose a turquoise, short-sleeved raw silk suit with a white lace blouse and white kid accessories. Kerry went into raptures over it. "You'll look terrific. Harrington doesn't realize what a lucky man he is."

Bryce rang up on Thursday night to make sure everything was going as planned. Caroline started telling him what she'd bought.

"Good, fine." He sounded distracted, disinterested, cold. It hurt badly.

"I'll see you on Saturday," she said, wanting to get away from him before she started crying.

"Yes. Please don't be late. I can't stand unpunctuality."

Chapter 14

Saturday dawned hot and sunny, a perfect February day. Andy arrived after lunch, hot and bothered, having hitchhiked from the base. After a cool shower and an even cooler beer, courtesy of Trevor, he soon regained his equilibrium.

"You've lost weight, Caro, and you're paler, too. I mean, this is what you want, isn't it? I don't want Harrington bullying you. Let me know if he does, and I'll deal with him." His handsome features were suddenly marred by a frown.

The nearer the time came for the nuptials, the more nervous Caroline became. She took a shower and Kerry helped her get dressed.

The two men whistled when they saw her.

"Wow! Harrington doesn't realize how lucky he is," Trevor said.

"You look lovely, Caro," Andy told her. "I've never seen you looking better."

"It's the best money can buy," she told him, trying not to sound cynical.

She had brushed her hair until it hung soft and silky about her shoulders. It was sun-bleached to pale blonde by now.

"If you're not happy about marrying him, there's still time to call it off," Andy said with a worried frown. "I can arrange with the army to pay you an allotment."

"I do want to marry him. Oh, I don't know." She forced a laugh because Andy was so anxious.

Kerry's frock was deep pink in color, a perfect foil for her black hair. Trevor wore a navy suit, Andy his uniform.

Bryce had organized a car for them, but by the time it arrived, ten minutes late, Caroline felt sick with anxiety.

"We're going to be late," Andy remarked.

"Too bad. It's not our fault," Kerry said. "Let

Harrington sweat it out a bit. He must have messed up the arrangements."

Bryce never messed up anything, except for getting her pregnant. He certainly wouldn't have planned that little episode. Caroline would stake her life on it. She grabbed Andy's hand and clung to it.

****

Bryce waited in the front of the chapel with his parents. He wore a dark suit with a white shirt. He glanced around the empty chapel. He could just about kill for a cigarette. Where was Caroline? They were late. If there was one thing he couldn't stand, it was tardiness. What if she jilted him at the altar? His stomach started churning.

His mother was wearing a floating chiffon dress in a pale peach color, with a cream hat and matching accessories. He had to admit that she was still a striking woman.

****

Iris Harrington sat in the front pew. She had come to the church under sufferance and had made no bones about it. Her lips were pursed as she waited for the bride to arrive. How Bryce, her own flesh and blood, could let a thing like this happen to him was beyond comprehension. Hadn't she presented him with some of the most socially eligible girls in Melbourne? He thumbed his nose at them, only to be trapped into marriage by some insignificant little typist.

It wasn't fair. How would she face her friends over their morning cocktails? The humiliation! This little office worker had even dared to cast aspersions on Bryce's suitability as a husband. Any slight against her flesh and blood Iris took as a personal insult. As for this hole-in-the-corner wedding, it was degrading. Didn't Bryce once describe Caroline Dennison as a prim little mouse? He was probably having this quiet, secretive little ceremony because he felt ashamed of her. This thought gave her a grim satisfaction.

Of course, the marriage could be dissolved after the child's birth. Maybe that's what he planned. Unlike Bryce to let anyone force his hand. Yes, that must be it. She felt relieved that the Harringtons were in complete control of the situation. Just as it should be.

****

Alexander Harrington sat next to his wife in the front row of the church.

He glanced at her several times but couldn't read what was going on in her mind. Plenty of conflicting thoughts, if the changing expression on her face was any indication. He wore a lightweight gray suit with a blue shirt and his favorite tie. This should have been a happy occasion, but Bryce looked positively savage as he sat on the edge of the pew.

He glanced around the chapel. Yes, the old place brought back a lot of memories. He had been married here himself, and he hoped the child would be a boy so it could attend here, too. He rather fancied the idea of seeing the principal and enrolling his grandson.

He smiled at the pleasant thoughts swirling around in his head. If it was a girl, she could attend the girls' college that now formed part of this college setup. Iris had gone there, as had the daughters of most of his friends. Would any of them know Caroline?

He could just picture himself walking into his club with his grandson trotting beside him. He had become heartily sick of some of his business friends boasting about their grandchildren, ramming their various exploits down his throat all the time. In a while it would be his turn. He savored the thought like vintage wine.

****

Bryce sat staring straight ahead.

If they didn't hurry, he would get up and walk out and damn the lot of them. He clenched his fist in his coat pocket. Why couldn't people smoke in church? It wasn't as if he intended to drop ash on the carpet or anything.

He glanced at Russell, who had been one of his closest friends at school. Imagine old Russ becoming a minister, married, with a couple of kids, too. Damn Caroline! This waiting was driving him crazy.

He glanced around the chapel and his eyes fastened on the Honor Rolls along one wall. He perused the names under 1914-18 and spotted Dennison three times. Probably Caroline's relations. Two had been killed in action apparently, as they had gold stars beside their names.

His eyes settled on the 1939-45 roll. Dennison appeared twice, with stars against both names. Andrew Dennison had won a bravery award. What a tragedy! Two generations of the family virtually wiped out by war. He felt proud that the name Harrington also appeared there.

He had never given much thought to the war, but he remembered his father saying he'd fought in the Middle East and the Pacific. Not that he ever spoke much about the war. He was in fact quite reticent about it, although his mother said the old man was an officer. Damn it, where the hell was Caroline?

The Harringtons had donated an honor board for students serving in Vietnam, and already there were a few names on it. Only one had a star against his name, though.

Captain Simon Alford. Poor old Fatty. They hadn't been close friends, but their lockers were next to each other in the last two years at school. Everyone called Simon "Fatty" not because he was fat but because he was so thin. Even in the fourth form he stood over six feet tall.

Bryce glanced towards the door again. Still no sign of them. He looked at his watch. Fifteen minutes late. He'd give them a piece of his mind when they arrived. That young Andy probably thought it amusing to have him cooling his heels. He wasn't a patient man—he would be the first to admit it—but this would try the patience of a saint.

He was just debating the legal ramifications if he got up and walked out, when Russell said quietly, "They're here."

He stood up on Russell's signal. Chancing a quick glance over his shoulder, he saw Kerry and Trevor. What was she doing here? If ever a female got his back up, it was her. Bad enough getting married, but having her here—he didn't know how Trevor put up with such a shrew.

He watched as the two of them took a seat on the opposite side of the church from him. Where the hell was Caroline? No wonder she was late. Kerry had probably instigated a delay on purpose. He didn't much care what Caroline did after their marriage, but Kerry was one female he didn't want her associating with.

At last he heard Russell say, "She's arrived."

"About time," Bryce snapped, before he could stop himself. He chanced a glance over his shoulder, watching his mother crane her neck.

Young Dennison certainly looked well in his uniform. What a fine, upstanding boy. A shaft of sunlight bouncing off one of the stained-glass windows momentarily enveloped him in a ghostly aura.

Bryce felt a cold rush of dread. This boy would soon be heading off to the jungles of Vietnam. Was his name destined to appear on the honor board with a star against it, like poor Fatty? *Get a grip on yourself, man.* He forced his emotions under control again.

He didn't know why, but he wanted to watch his bride walking down the aisle. What was wrong with him? Why should he care what she looked like? He argued with himself, *I'm only marrying her because I have no choice.* Doing the honorable thing, as men of his father's generation would say.

When Caroline was nearly up to him, he glanced over his shoulder again and caught his breath. She looked exquisite. Her hair was very blonde, thanks to the sun. Her huge eyes were over-bright, her skin white and smooth as porcelain. She started trembling. He knew he should smile, give her some kind of encouragement, but he couldn't. Damn it all, she had kept him waiting, hadn't she?

Suddenly she baulked. Andy had to almost push her to Bryce's side. She acted like a scared rabbit. Russell started the service. It was brief, just the bare necessities. Bryce had warned Russ to cut out all the usual sentimental mumbo-jumbo.

He fumbled in his pocket for the ring and laid it on the Bible to be blessed. When it came time to slip the ring on Caroline's finger, her hand shook. He was shocked to notice a fine tremor to his own hand, also.

"I now pronounce you man and wife."

Thank goodness. It was all over. Just a couple of signatures, and that would be the end of it. It suddenly registered that Russell was staring at him with a weird expression on his face.

"You may now kiss the bride." He repeated the words slowly, distinctly.

"What? Oh, of course." Bryce put his hands on Caroline's shoulders and brushed her lips with his own. Russell gave him another strange look. What was wrong with him? Did Russell expect him to take Caroline in his arms and kiss her properly? He had to be kidding, although the proposition wasn't as abhorrent as he wanted to make out. In fact...

They trouped out to the vestry to sign the register. His parents, Andy, Kerry and Trevor came, too, and he introduced everyone. He noticed his mother scrutinizing Caroline, desperate to find some flaw in her appearance. He grinned to himself. His mother was being her typical snobbish self. He didn't know why, but he felt pleased with Caroline's appearance. She'd picked her outfit well. Not showy or outrageous, just understated good taste.

"Well, my dear." Bryce watched his father come up to Caroline. "You'll have to call me Dad from now on." He kissed her cheek. "I always wanted a daughter, and now I've got one." He was the happiest person in the vestry, no question about it.

"How are you, Caroline?" His mother spoke in aristocratic tones. She used different voices for different occasions. "You can call me Iris. Now, you're Andrew, aren't you?" She turned towards the young captain.

"Yes, my friends call me Andy, but you can call me Andrew."

Bryce winced, but his mother didn't pick up the snub.

"Well, my boy, you've done it." His father came up and slapped him on the back, completely overdoing the jocularity bit. "I've booked a table for us at Sebastian's."

"You what?" His mother took the words right out of his mouth.

"We have to celebrate. You'll come won't you, Kerry, Trevor?"

"No, thanks, Mr. Harrington. We can't stay. We have to go out. We only wanted to give Caro some moral support." Kerry answered, shooting Bryce a triumphant smile.

"What a shame you've got a prior engagement," he drawled, lying through his teeth. He caught Kerry's eye and could see she knew damn well he was glad they weren't coming.

He watched them kiss Caroline goodbye, shake hands with everyone else and prepare to leave.

"May I kiss the groom?" Kerry smirked up at him, and Bryce found himself grinding his teeth. Because his father and everyone else seemed to expect it, he touched her lips briefly with his own.

"I expect to be godmother," she said, firing one last parting shot.

He almost choked with rage. She would have to be the most infuriating female God ever put breath into.

They trouped outside to the car. The Jaguar was roomy enough for the five of them to fit in comfortably. Bryce drove to the restaurant and parked in the car park. This was a basement restaurant, exclusive, one of his father's favorites.

Caroline's hand felt icy cold when he touched it. He stared into her face, and her pallor worried him. "You okay?" He didn't mean to sound abrupt, but it came out that way.

"Yes."

"If you want to be sick, just say so."

"I won't disgrace you, if that's what you're worried about." She sounded weary, somehow sad.

"I wasn't worrying about that. I'm worried about you." It was true. He couldn't explain why, but he did feel anxious about her welfare. "If you're not well, we can give this farcical wedding feast a miss."

"You okay, Sis? You look crook."

Bryce watched his mother wince.

"Don't they teach you to speak correctly at the Military Academy, Andrew?" She didn't even try to hide her disdain.

They were walking down the steps by this time. Bryce wondered if his father would be all right. Hadn't he read somewhere about steps being bad for heart victims? But his father didn't look like he had a worry in the world. He was enjoying himself. *Only one who is*, Bryce thought bitterly.

They arrived inside the foyer of the restaurant. It was cool and dim, and Bryce felt grateful for the dimness.

"My son has just got married, and this is his pretty bride," his father announced, and Bryce could have sunk through the floor. Every head in the restaurant swiveled towards them.

They were escorted to a table set with a white lacy tablecloth. Red candles in carved silver holders gave out a soft flickering glow. He held the chair out for Caroline, suppressing a smirk as he saw Andy doing the same for his mother.

"Just a little something we learned at the Academy."

"Andy, stop it," Caroline admonished him. "He's only teasing Mrs., um, I mean, Iris."

They had seafood crepes for an appetizer and pork fillets with sour cream as their main course. Two bottles of champagne rested in silver, ice-filled buckets. There was also a dish of chicken fillets, floured and grilled, and fresh garden salad. Bryce watched Caroline eat all of her meal. He didn't know why, but it pleased him. Of course, he didn't want her being sick. Pregnant women needed to eat to stay healthy; that must have been why he felt glad. Now that the formalities were over, he felt quite hungry himself. The food tasted superb, as always.

Dessert consisted of brandy-snap baskets filled with glazed wild berries.

Bryce, mellowed by the food, smilingly encouraged Caroline to eat the delicious fare.

"Caro." Andy tapped her on the hand. "I don't want to spoil the evening, but this time next week I could be in Vietnam."

Four spoons dropped with a clatter into the dessert bowls.

"No, you can't. Please, Andy," she implored, grabbing his hand. "You'll get killed."

"Better a dead hero than a live coward."

There was a sudden shocked silence. Giving a strangled sob, Caroline got up from the table and fled.

"Hell," Bryce exploded. "Couldn't you have kept your mouth shut for a while longer? She was enjoying her food."

"Where else could I tell her? I only found out last night."

"Go after her, son. She's upset," his father urged.

"You should comfort her."

"Yes, go after her. You're her husband," Andy put in.

"Oh, great." Bryce's lip curled. "You surely don't expect me to go into the ladies' powder room?"

"You could wait for her near the entrance," Andy retorted.

"And get arrested for being some kind of pervert? You wait for her, if you want to run the risk." He gulped down his champagne.

"Go and check on her, Iris. She's in shock—she might have collapsed," Bryce heard his father say.

Collapsed? He hadn't thought of that. "For God's sake, Mother, go and check on her. Pregnant women faint, don't they?" He turned worried eyes on his father.

"Don't ask me. I wouldn't know. Your mother has never fainted in her entire life."

"For heaven's sake," his mother said frigidly. "I'll go. Then we are leaving. This farce has gone on for long enough. I'll never be able to hold my head up again. Never, I tell you." She glared at Andy.

"Don't look at me. And don't blame Caroline, either. It's your son's fault." He scowled at Bryce, who savaged him with just one look.

"Ah, she's coming," he heard his father say.

"You okay, Caro? I'm sorry for blurting it out like that." Andy put his arm around her shoulder.

That's my role, Bryce thought furiously. I'm the one who should be comforting her. He couldn't help noticing how pale and stricken she looked.

"I suggest we go," he said, getting up and removing Andy's arm from Caroline. He didn't know why he had a strong desire to knock it off, but he did manage to restrain himself.

"I'll get the bill," Bryce said, watching his father link one of his arms through Caroline's and the other through his mother's before heading towards the door.

"I will see you before you go back, won't I?" Caroline asked Andy in a fear-filled voice as they prepared to leave.

"No. I'm being picked up at five o'clock in the morning." He grinned, and Bryce wondered how he could act so cheerful when he was marching off to war.

"I'll give you a ring in a couple of days. Give me your home phone number, Harrington."

Andy moved away, and Bryce followed him.

"Here." Bryce pulled out a business card, wrote his private number on it and handed it to Andy.

"Thanks. I won't be back before I go. All leave is cancelled."

"I had a feeling it might be."

"The army is worried about antiwar protesters stirring up trouble," Andy told him.

"Understandable. Ranting lunatics, most of them."

"I don't want to upset Caroline again, but if I haven't rung by Wednesday, it means I've either gone or can't get to a phone."

"All right. Good luck."

"Who needs luck? I'll probably spend my tour of duty at our base camp in Nui Dat."

Bryce dropped his parents off first.

"Good luck, Andrew." Alexander shook his hand. "You give those Viet Cong the hiding they deserve," he said fiercely. "Show them what the Aussie soldier is made of."

"Yes, good luck, Andrew." Bryce watched his mother bestow a benevolent smile on him. A young soldier going off to war tugged at the heartstrings. His mother would get plenty of mileage out of that at her committee meetings. Like a vampire let loose in a blood bank, she'd suck out every drop.

"Bring Caroline over one day soon. I'll search out my old school photos. Sure to be some of her father." Alexander leaned through the open window and kissed Caroline's cheek.

"Thank you, I'd like that. I haven't got any pictures of Dad."

They drove off and were soon pulling up outside Caroline's apartment. Bryce watched with narrowed eyes as Caroline kissed Andy goodbye.

"Take care, Sis." He ruffled her hair and gave her a hug. "Look after her, Harrington, and make sure you treat her decently."

"I will." Bryce got out of the car and shook Andy's hand. "Good luck. If you need anything, just let me know."

They drove away in silence. Bryce was morose, brooding, and Caroline felt sad and frightened. Bryce had seemed so angry during the ceremony, even if he did thaw out over dinner. She knew he regretted his decision to marry her. Maybe he would want a divorce after a couple of months. She had to stop this incessant weeping, but it was hard, knowing that your husband had only married you because he felt duty-bound to do so, and on top of that your brother was marching off to war.

Chapter 15

It was nine o'clock by the time they arrived at his apartment. Bryce parked the car, and they alighted. Caroline stood without speaking while he locked the doors. He was always so security conscious. With his hand under her arm, he escorted her to the elevator, then down the hall when they reached his floor.

At the door of his apartment, she faltered.

"Come on." He flung the door open. She was probably remembering the last time she was here. *Who isn't?* He didn't know why, but he scooped her up in his arms and carried her across the threshold, kicking the door shut behind them. He lowered her to the ground, watching as she stood there, uncertainty written all over her face.

"Come on, for heaven's sake. This is your home now. Stop acting like a frightened rabbit."

"I think mouse was the word you once used to describe me."

"Would you like a cup of tea? I'll make you one, if you like."

"That's my job, isn't it? I'll have to earn my keep somehow."

Her lips trembled, and he knew he should comfort her but couldn't bring himself to do it. *I've done the right thing. I've married her. What more did she expect?* He was acting like a self-righteous pig, but he resented being maneuvered into doing something he didn't want to do.

"I feel tired. I might go straight to bed."

Was she dropping hints? No, of course not. She looked exhausted, and so sad it smote his heart.

"Do that. Why not have a bath or a shower?" He hoped he sounded kind rather than autocratic.

"Could I? I mean, have a bath in that swimming pool in the bathroom?"

"Why not? It will relax you."

"Thanks. It's been a trying day."

God, what an understatement. He just stopped himself in time from saying the words outloud.

****

Caroline walked towards the bedroom and Bryce followed.

"I think I might change my clothes, too," he said. "I've just about cooked all afternoon. I feel like a trussed-up Christmas turkey."

"If you want a shower, you can use the bathroom first," she offered tentatively. Did he expect to use the bathroom at the same time as her? He was her husband now and had the right, if he wanted to exercise it.

He must have read her mind. "You have your bath; I won't disturb you. I'll have a shower later."

She followed him into the bedroom, where he opened the wardrobe and pulled out a pair of shorts and a T-shirt.

There was special heating inside his wardrobe to keep the creases out of the clothes, Caroline noticed as she stood beside him.

"I've moved some of my gear out so you can have the top three drawers."

"Thanks for hanging my clothes up, but I could have done it."

He looked shocked. "I didn't unpack your clothes. I got my housekeeper to do it. They would have ended up in a jumbled heap if it was left to me."

"I'll try and make you a good wife—just tell me what you expect."

"I don't expect anything. You can go your way, I'll go mine, and we'll get along quite well."

He stripped off his coat and she watched as he took off his shirt. She couldn't drag her eyes away from his tanned, muscular chest. Once she had buried her face in that mat of hair, she thought sadly, wondering whether she would ever do so again. What if he took up with his other women? The thought sickened her.

After unbuckling his belt, he started unzipping his trousers.

"We're married now, so you can look if you like, Miss Prim—or rather, Mrs. Prim." He laughed at her embarrassment. "You can turn around now. I'm decently covered."

She couldn't decide whether he was teasing her or not.

"Sort out what you need for bed, and I'll bring you a cup of tea in a while," he said before sauntering off.

Caroline waited until he'd left the room before going to one of the drawers and taking out a neatly folded negligee set. The calf-length black silk nightgown had slits halfway up either side, with a top of lacy net that plunged to a deep V between her breasts.

Why had she let Kerry talk her into buying such a vampish thing? The other part of the set was in the same silky material but only had lace trimming around the edges.

In the bathroom, she turned on the taps and started to fill the bath. This bathroom was the last word in luxury. If only Bryce loved her and Andy wasn't going to Vietnam, she would be the happiest person in the world.

She found a bottle of rose-scented bath salts. It wouldn't belong to Bryce, and she wondered who owned it. One of his many lady friends, she thought bitterly, tempted to throw it into the garbage. When she removed the lid she discovered, to her relief, that the inside was still sealed. It had never been used. Maybe the housekeeper had bought it.

What would she do about the housekeeper? If she didn't go out to work, she needed something to fill in the time. Maybe they could compromise. She could do some of the work and let the housekeeper do the heavier tasks.

Caroline relaxed in the water, letting the warmth flow over her. Such luxury! She could have stayed there for hours.

"Hey, are you all right?" Hard knuckles rapped against the door. "What on earth are you doing in there? I thought you must have drowned."

"Sorry! It felt so relaxing, I forgot the time."

"Your tea is ready."

Reluctantly she climbed out of the bath, patting herself dry on a huge fluffy towel. She slipped into the nightdress and matching robe and, after giving her hair a quick brush, padded out to the kitchen.

Bryce sat at the island bar, reading a sporting magazine.

"There's your tea." He pointed to a bone china cup and saucer. "Do you want something to eat? There should be some biscuits around somewhere."

"No, thanks, just the tea."

His gaze wandered from her feet to her throat, until it finally rested on her breasts. Could he see the shadowy outline of her nipples? Her stomach muscles tightened.

"Your mother doesn't like me. She thinks I'm not good enough for you."

He gave a careless shrug. "My mother is a first-class snob. You wouldn't appeal to her because your name doesn't appear in the social columns. Of course, you could always join her chicken-and-champagne lunches, maybe help out at some fundraiser or other, and then you'd be in the clique with a vengeance."

"I don't happen to like those kinds of things. It's all so fake. You wouldn't want me to go to them, would you?"

He laughed. "You're priceless. I don't expect you to do anything you don't want to do, and believe me—" He grimaced. "That would be the last kind of function I'd ask you to attend."

When they had finished their drinks, Caroline took the cups and was about to rinse them.

"Put them in the dishwasher. Mrs. Evans, my housekeeper, waits until the machine is full before turning it on."

"Oh?" Caroline felt so inept. It would take ages for her to adjust to being the wife of a rich man, if she ever did. *You're not destined for great things, Caroline, not like your brother,* her mother used to say. *You're just ordinary.* She could never understand why her mother had chosen to denigrate her all the time. Or why she burnt every picture of their father. She had refused to talk about him, as if she never wanted to admit that he ever existed.

"I think I might go to bed now."

"You do that. I want to finish reading this." He waved a car magazine in front of her.

Caroline dawdled towards the bedroom. She didn't know what else to do.

****

Bryce knew Caroline was upset. He saw the hurt in her eyes. She needed comfort, but he felt so inadequate.

As he watched her walk slowly away, a dispirited droop to her shoulders, he had a strange, almost overwhelming desire to call her back, but he didn't.

I've married her, haven't I? He tried to excuse his boorish behavior. *I'm behaving like a pig.* What was wrong with him, anyway? He'd hurt her on purpose. He flung the magazine down. He hadn't read a word, anyway. Stalking into the sitting room, he switched on the television.

He puffed moodily on a cigarette but after only a few puffs stubbed it out in the ashtray. A second-rate western had appeared on the screen. When he could stand it no longer, he turned the dial, only to be confronted by some torrid love scene. That he could certainly do without. Sporting repeats on another channel did nothing for him. In the end he turned it off in disgust.

To hell with it. He would go to bed. He was tired. It had been one hell of a day. After all, it is my bed, isn't it? He was being unreasonable—bloody idiotic, in fact—but couldn't seem to stop himself, just the same. It was a desperate form of self-preservation.

He wandered into the bathroom and took a shower. Would he shave? No, he couldn't be bothered, even though his five-o'clock shadow rasped when he rubbed his knuckles over his jaw.

He returned to the bedroom, where one of the side lamps had been left on. He flicked it off, shrugged out of his robe and slipped under the sheet. Caroline lay on the far side of the bed. He thought for a moment that she might be asleep, but then he realized she was sobbing into her pillow.

He should reach out, take her in his arms and offer her some comfort, but he couldn't. He rolled over, pummeling the pillow with his fist. Why was he so angry with her?

On remembering what had transpired the last time they shared this bed, he almost yelled out in frustration.

"Can't you sleep, Bryce?" He felt her hand on his bare shoulder.

"Yes, I can sleep. Just leave me alone."

"I'm sorry," she whispered.

"Sorry? You're sorry?" He vented his anger and

uncertainty on her. "You've got nothing to be sorry about. You've landed yourself a rich husband and can laugh all the way to the bank. I'm the one who's sorry. I'm saddled with a wife and kid I don't want."

He felt the shudder go through her even as she moved away from him, and he could have bitten his tongue out. There had been no need to attack her. It was his fault. This whole sordid, bloody mess was his fault entirely. She was young and innocent, he a mature, experienced man who should have known better. He'd used his penis instead of his brain, and now he had to put up with the consequences.

He pummeled the pillow again. He lay there for a time and could tell by her breathing that Caroline had fallen asleep. Some wedding night. He tossed and turned for a while. God, he felt tired, but he was so overwrought he didn't think he would ever sleep soundly again.

Bryce awoke some time later. He switched the bedside lamp on, and as he glanced at the clock he suppressed a groan. Three o'clock. He moved his leg and came in contact with something warm and soft, so he rolled over. Caroline lay on her side, facing him, her hair cascading all over the pillow.

She looked angelic, her well-shaped lips slightly parted. Her skin was pure white, silky soft, as he trailed his fingers across her cheek. She didn't stir. He traced the line of her jaw and felt need surge through him. This couldn't be happening. He wanted her with a fierce desire that was killing in its intensity.

He ran his hands down over her body. He couldn't drag his gaze from her cleavage, and he ached to touch her nipples with his tongue. Continuing his gentle exploration, he fumed because his touch was restricted by her nightgown. He felt like ripping it off and throwing it away. Come to that, he'd like to throw all her nightgowns away. She didn't need them. Better for her to sleep naked, as he did. That's how nature intended it to be.

Burying his face in her hair, he savored the smell and texture of it. He groaned in frustration as his need started to become urgent, his erection harder. He pushed the straps of her nightgown down and let his finger slide along the smooth valley. Cupping a breast in either hand he drew the creamy mounds together, encircling both nipples with his tongue.

He shouldn't wake her up, not after being such a bastard last night, but he hadn't meant all those things he said. He was upset, confused. Surely she would realize that.

They were husband and wife now, and he desperately wanted to consummate their marriage. So it wasn't a love match, and he resented the thought of being tied down to one woman, but regular, hot sex with someone as warm and generous as Caroline would be great compensation.

"Caroline, Caroline," he groaned her name over and over. God, how he wanted her—his whole body ached with desire.

He recalled hearing or reading about pregnant women needing plenty of rest. Well, she could rest all day tomorrow, but he wanted her now, and his desire was becoming more urgent as every second passed.

"Wake up, darling. I want you, need you." He nibbled her earlobe until she stirred.

****

Carolyn woke up to the feel of Bryce's hot mouth against her throat. It hadn't been a dream. It really was him. "What are you doing?"

"I'm making love to you. I know I should let you sleep, but I can't."

His mouth clamping over hers stilled her reply. She felt the pressure of his tongue between her lips, the thrust of his hardening maleness against her thigh. Bryce didn't love her, but he wanted her, and for now that was enough.

She listened to him groaning with need, sensed his fierce desire and smelt the musky scent of his arousal. She parted her legs and he drove into her with one long, powerful stroke.

Moving slowly at first, rhythmically, faster and faster, building up the tempo, he laved her love canal until it fluttered into life, yielding, sensitive, eagerly responsive to his every movement. He drew back. She sobbed in deprivation, raking her fingers across his back in frustrated desperation.

Giving a feral growl, he drove into her again, hard and deep. The yielding flesh of her arousal, nurtured into pulsating life by him, closed around his velvet shaft, enfolding it as he worked his magic.

"Bryce," Caroline cried out his name as she reached her climax. Her back instinctively arched, her hips levitated.

Just as he reached the pinnacle of his orgasm, Bryce's whole body shuddered and he exploded inside her. They collapsed in a heap of tangled limbs and sheets, their sweat-slicked bodies fused together.

"My God, Caroline," he gasped. "You're really something."

Too overcome to speak, too exhausted to move, all she could do was run trembling fingers across his cheek.

****

Next morning Caroline woke to the sounds of crockery and a grinning Bryce bearing a breakfast tray.

"Good morning, Mrs. Harrington. Sleep well?"

Her cheeks burned. "Yes, thank you," she answered primly, trying to hitch the sheet up over her breasts as she sat up.

"Don't cover them, they're beautiful." He leaned across to kiss each rosy tip. "I've eaten breakfast and been for a run. What would you like to do today?"

"Stay in bed." She felt too comfortable and satiated to move.

He laughed, and what a difference it made to him. "You're a brazen hussy." He wagged a finger at her. "Dad rang a while ago, wanting to know if we'd like to come over for lunch. They always have a traditional Sunday roast. It's going to be hot, and we could use the pool afterwards."

"Sounds nice. Do you always go there on Sunday?"

"Sometimes I do."

Had he taken Amanda, Shereen or another from his bevy of beauties for a Sunday roast?

He frowned and she wondered whether he guessed the thoughts and questions running through her mind.

"I go, sometimes. Depends on what I'm doing. Dad found those old school photos he told you about."

"Let's go, then. You know, I can't remember ever having seen a picture of my father."

"Your mother—surely she kept some."

"She burnt them all."

"What a shame. Why?"

"Who knows? Mum grew increasingly bitter about being left a widow with two little kids. I think she blamed my father for getting himself killed."

"He was a hero. Dad said he won a swag of bravery medals."

"I know. She was a strange woman. I didn't realize until I got older exactly how strange. I think she was jealous. Didn't want us to love Dad, only her. Well, she didn't care about me, but Andy was her shining star."

"I'm sorry."

She shrugged, but her mother's rejection still hurt. "Oh, she wasn't cruel, I mean, abusive. She didn't starve or beat me. She just didn't like me and made no effort to hide it. Did you have a happy childhood?" she asked, biting into a piece of toast.

"I suppose so. Well, Dad was affectionate and spent every spare minute he could with me, but he was busy building up the business."

"Your mother?"

"A social butterfly. She didn't spend much time with me. Always flitting around from one charity function to another. She's not very maternal."

"Our baby won't suffer like that." Her hand went to pat her stomach. "I'll tell it a dozen times a day how much I love it," she declared fiercely.

"Me too," he said, walking over to the window and drawing the drapes back. "It's ten-thirty."

"Ten-thirty?" She jumped out of bed and the dreaded nausea rose up in her throat. Dashing to the bathroom, she lost her breakfast in the toilet bowl.

"Are you all right?" Bryce handed her a towel. "Did I expect too much last night? I mean..."

"No, sudden movements in the morning or certain smells set me off. It has nothing to do with last night."

He hovered near her. "I'm a selfish person. I've only ever considered myself, but if I ever ask too much of you, tell me."

"It was wonderful last night, better than I ever dreamed it could be." She rose to her feet, purposely turning her back on the mirror. No point in seeing exactly how awful she looked.

"Did, did you enjoy it?" she asked huskily.

"Yes, you know I did. It was the best sex I've ever had. When I lit the right fuse, you went off like a firecracker."

No words of love, but Bryce enjoyed the sex. Better than nothing. Love came with children. That's what people said about arranged marriages. She remembered reading that somewhere.

"Have a shower, and then we'll go," he suggested. "Dad was so excited because he found the old school photographs of your father. He can't wait to show them to you."

Caroline dressed in a white linen slack suit. The red cowl-neck top suited her. She had never worn red silk before. Bryce wore navy trousers and a blue-and-white, geometric-design shirt.

"Should we bring something with us?" she asked.

"There's no need."

"Flowers for your mother?"

"No, they won't expect anything."

"Do I look all right?"

He snorted in exasperation. "Of course you do. I'd tell you if you didn't."

"I'm sorry." She touched his arm. "I just want to make a good impression."

"You will, so stop worrying. You'll end up with ulcers before you're thirty."

She couldn't help feeling insecure, inadequate. Her mother had made sure of that. The Harringtons belonged to the "beautiful people" brigade. Wealthy, articulate, good-looking. Everything she wasn't.

Chapter 16

They pulled up in front of the Harrington mansion, and Caroline's anxiety escalated. "You look gorgeous," Bryce said, helping her from the car with his usual hand under the elbow. "You know, I've always liked this view of the house best. It looks so elegant set at the end of such a long sweeping drive."

"Yes, you could almost believe you were in the country. You can't even see your neighbors. It must have been wonderful growing up in such a place."

"It was. I learnt to ride my first bike on the lawns over there. Dad thought the grass would cushion my fall if I fell off." He laughed. "I'd have been black and blue otherwise." He took her hand and squeezed it reassuringly as they walked towards the house.

"Mrs. Ferguson, this is my wife, Caroline," Bryce said, introducing her to the housekeeper who met them at the door. "Mrs. Ferguson is the best cook in Melbourne."

"Ah, Mr. Harrington." She chuckled. "Ever the flatterer. I'm pleased to meet you, Mrs. Harrington."

"Nice to meet you, too, Mrs. Ferguson."

With trepidation, Caroline entered the house. Persian carpet on the floor, frescoed ceilings, chandeliers and antique furniture, all just as she'd imagined it would be. She was so overcome with nerves that she baulked.

"Come on." Bryce's hand in the small of her back propelled her forward.

They entered a sitting room as opulent as the other rooms she had glanced into.

"Ah, Caroline." Alexander came towards her, arms outstretched. "How are you, my dear?" He gave her a hug.

"I'm very well, thanks. How are you?"

"All the better for seeing a pretty young thing like you. How's it going, son?"

"I'm fine. Where's Mother?"

"Fluttering around as usual. I found the school

photos I told you about. Have a seat next to me on the couch, Caroline. A drink?"

"No, thanks."

"Caroline was sick this morning."

"Oh, my dear, I'm so sorry."

"Morning sickness, no big deal."

"I remember when Iris was pregnant with Bryce. She spent the best part of an hour each morning with her head down the toilet."

"Alexander," Iris snapped, as she minced into the room. Caroline stifled a giggle, trying to visualize this haughty queen with her head stuck in the toilet bowl.

"I found peppermint tea helpful. Would you care for some?"

"No, thank you. It's just sudden movements or spicy smells that tend to set me off in the morning. Otherwise I'm okay."

"Pregnant women need plenty of rest." Iris went on, and Caroline felt her cheeks burn. She lowered her head, letting her hair hide most of her face. Surely Iris couldn't tell that they had spent half the night making love.

"It was their wedding night." Alexander chuckled, and Caroline, through a curtain of hair, watched Bryce squirm in his seat.

"Where are the photos you wanted to show Caroline?" he butted in hurriedly, giving her the distinct impression that he was embarrassed. Could his father suspect how prolonged and vigorous their lovemaking had been in the early hours of the morning?

"Now, my dear. This is the football team of 1934. We were premiers that year. There's your father."

Caroline stared at the smiling young man and instantly saw why her mother had disliked her—she was the spitting image of him.

"You're so like your father," Alexander said. "I can't understand why I didn't recognize you. The old eyes aren't as sharp as they used to be, and memory isn't, either."

"Is that you?" Caroline pointed to another grinning young man.

"Yes." He gave a chuckle. "Haven't I changed much, or did you pick me out because of Bryce?"

It was the latter, but she couldn't say so. "You

haven't changed a bit," she teased. "Still as handsome as a movie star."

Iris snorted, but Caroline didn't care. He was a nice old man, if a little on the vain side.

"No fool like an old fool," Iris said tartly. "Alexander," she raised her voice.

"We're just going to the drawing room," Bryce said. "I want to see mother's Fundraiser of the Year award."

"Well, of course, darling," Caroline heard Iris say. "It's a biennial award presented by the governor's wife."

"Yes, I know how prestigious it is. What an honor for you." Bryce took hold of his mother's arm and steered her out of the room.

"I'll see if I can get some pictures taken off these snaps," Alexander promised. "I'm only sorry I don't have any more to show you."

"It was kind of you to go to so much trouble. Until today, I didn't even know what my father looked like," Caroline said wistfully.

"I'll make some enquiries, if you like. On enlistment every soldier has his photo taken. There should be one of your father on his military records. You might be able to get it enlarged."

"That would be wonderful, thank you. You know I love your son, don't you?"

"Yes. I see it in your eyes, the way you speak to him, touch him."

"He doesn't love me," she whispered sadly.

"I wouldn't be so sure about that, but if he doesn't now, he soon will," Alexander reassured. "You make a nice welcoming home for him, don't be afraid to show your affection, and he'll soon come around, I guarantee it. Don't be worrying about your brother, either." He patted her hand. "He's a smart young man, well trained and disciplined, knows how to look after himself."

"I hope so."

"I know so. You take it from an old soldier. I sneaked in a few of Bryce's baby photos. Thought you might be interested."

"Oh, yes. What a gorgeous baby!" She stared at the photo of an infant Bryce wearing a long, lacy dress.

"I took that picture at his baptism."

"Look at this one." She pointed to the photo of Bryce as a toddler riding a rocking horse.

"What mischief are you two plotting?" Bryce came up to them.

"Your father's been showing me a few of your baby pictures."

"Dad! Caroline wouldn't be interested in that old rubbish."

"I am. You were a beautiful baby and a handsome little boy."

"Mother sent me in to tell you lunch is ready."

Caroline stood up. "Thank you for showing me the photographs. They were wonderful." She tossed her hair back and pushed it behind her ears.

"Don't push you hair back," Bryce said, hurriedly stepping between her and his father.

"Why ever not?"

"Because you've got a love bite on your neck," he shot back in a loud whisper

"I didn't notice." She felt embarrassed heat rushing into her face as Alexander mumbled something before walking away.

"Don't you look in the mirror?"

"Not much." How could she tell him she rarely did more than glance in the mirror to apply lipstick.

"Don't let my mother see it. I've already endured the third degree."

"What about?"

"Us." His mouth grew tight.

"You mean she asked you…"

"More or less."

"Oh, no." Caroline could almost feel herself breaking out in a cold sweat. "What did you say?" She clutched his arm.

"I told her to mind her own damn business."

She gritted her teeth, forcing her trembling legs into motion. What kind of woman was Iris Harrington, asking her son about his wedding night? Now they had to share a meal together.

She plastered a smile on her face, patted her hair to make sure it covered the love bite and entered the dining room. The table was set up for royalty, all gleaming silver and crisp white linen.

Alexander sat at the head of the table carving the leg of lamb. The table was laden with bowls of crisp roast potatoes, pumpkin, carrots, onions, beans and peas, and thick brown gravy, and Caroline feared she wouldn't be able to swallow so much as a mouthful.

Under the eagle eye of a tight-lipped Iris, she tried to do justice to the beautiful meal. That mother and son had argued was obvious, not that it seemed to affect the older woman's appetite. She ate heartily, having ruined the meal for everyone else. How could a nice, warm-hearted man like Alexander have married an ice queen like her?

"I've decided to have a post-wedding party for our special friends."

"Forget it," Bryce snapped.

"The Fontains were so hurt at not being invited to the wedding, and they're such close friends. Ashley became distraught after talking to you yesterday morning."

Caroline felt icy cold with dread. Ashley Fontain was the girl Iris had wanted Bryce to marry.

"Don't you ever give up? I'm a married man."

"Only under sufferance."

"For God's sake, Mother."

"There's always divorce."

"Iris!" Alexander admonished her with just the one word.

"After a decent interval, I mean. Bryce would pay you handsomely for your, um, trouble, Caroline."

"Trouble?" Caroline leapt to her feet. "Your grandchild is trouble?" she screamed. "You evil, hateful old witch." She marched up to her mother-in-law.

Iris got to her feet, trembling with rage. "How dare you! You, you ungrateful little guttersnipe."

Caroline heard a sudden gurgling sound and swung around in time to see Alexander topple to the floor clutching his chest.

"Hell!" Bryce dashed over to his stricken father. "Call an ambulance, quickly."

Caroline sprinted to the phone and dialed the emergency number.

The next few minutes would stick in her mind

forever. While Bryce knelt down next to his father, Iris paced up and down.

"This is all your fault, you little gold digger. Forcing my son into marriage. Ingratiating yourself with my husband. You dirty little trollop."

While Iris vilified her, Bryce said nothing to defend her, and Caroline knew for certain that their marriage was doomed. His face was chalk white, his lips drawn into a thin angry line. His eyes were dark with worry for his father and rightly so, but for her, his wife—nothing.

The ambulance arrived and the attendants stabilized Alexander, who had regained consciousness.

"What's all the fuss about? I don't need to go to hospital."

"Of course you do. I'll drop Caroline off at my apartment first, then bring mother to the hospital."

Drop Caroline off "at my apartment," Bryce had said, not "at home." She felt worse with every passing minute.

When the ambulance took off with its siren blaring, so did they. The ten-minute drive was silent, fraught with animosity. Caroline got relegated to the back seat while Iris reigned like a queen in the front next to Bryce.

"You don't need to drop me off. I'd like to go to the hospital, too."

"Stay away from my husband," Iris snapped, and Caroline could do nothing else but slump in her seat and keep her mouth shut.

Bryce escorted her up to the apartment and saw her inside. "Hey, I know you're upset. It was a hell of a shock for all of us. We'll talk things over when I get back. I don't know when that will be, though." He gave her quick, passionless kiss on the cheek, swung around on his heel and left.

Caroline's legs trembled so much they could barely support her weight. She somehow made it to the bathroom and vomited her heart out.

After washing her face and cleaning her teeth, she undressed and staggered into bed, where she lay shaking. The taste of vomit stuck in her throat, rank and sour, but it was nothing compared to the way she felt in her heart— hurt and betrayed.

Bryce had ignored his mother's vitriolic attack on

her. Of course he was worried and upset about his father, but at least he could have told his mother to shut up and stop assassinating his wife's character.

She curled up in the fetal position, moaning in anguish. Would Mr. Harrington be all right? *Please, God, help him. Help all of us*, she prayed desperately.

The bed felt cold, overlarge, without Bryce sharing it with her. Once he calmed down, would he still blame her for his father's collapse? Would it be one more obstacle for them to overcome?

****

Bryce didn't arrive home until four o'clock in the morning. She glanced at the clock when she heard him in the bathroom.

"How's your father?" she asked as he slid into bed.

"He's going to be okay, thank goodness. They'll keep him in for a couple of days for observation," he said with a weary sigh. "But it was a close call."

She wound her arms around his neck. "I'm sorry. I wouldn't hurt your father for the world."

"I know. We'll talk about it later. I need to get a few hours sleep before work."

"Take the day off."

"I can't, Geoff is away until Wednesday. Please, Caroline, don't badger me. I'm dog tired."

****

Just before eight o'clock Caroline got out of bed. Bryce still slept. His face was pale, his jaw covered with black stubble, and her heart bled. He looked exhausted. Still in her nightgown, she went out to the kitchen and turned on the percolator. She took a quick shower and dressed in jeans and a pink-and-white, candy-striped top.

Returning to the bedroom, she leaned over the bed and shook his shoulder. "It's nearly eight-thirty."

"What?" he said groggily, trying to focus his eyes. "I feel hellish."

"I know. I've got the percolator on. I'll cook you some breakfast while you take a shower."

"Just toast, thanks. I don't have time for anything else."

When Bryce came out to the kitchen fifteen minutes later, showered and shaved, Caroline's heart turned over.

Pale and drawn, he still looked impressive. Love welled up inside her, and she feared it would tumble out if she opened her mouth.

"I've rung the hospital and Dad spent a comfortable night."

"I'm glad."

She poured his coffee, and he propped himself at the island bar to drink it.

"Would it be okay if I visited your father?"

"I suppose so, as long as you don't go at the same time as my mother."

"She blames me for your father's attack, doesn't she?"

"Yes."

"And you? Do you blame me, too?"

"No, but you shouldn't have argued with her."

"She insulted me."

"You were a guest in her house. You should have..."

"You do blame me," she interrupted. "I would have put up with the insults to me, but not to our baby."

"Hell, I'm not in the mood to argue." He pushed his half-eaten toast away. "I've got to get to work."

"What am I going to do?"

"Whatever you like." He got up and strode towards the door. "Don't wait dinner for me. I'll grab a bite on my way to the hospital."

After he left she tidied up the apartment. She could have given it a thorough going over, even though it was clean, but didn't dare. No point in falling foul of Bryce's housekeeper. She had enough enemies without making a new one. Iris Harrington, Ashley Fontain and her parents—they all wanted to bring her down. She had landed in a nest of vipers.

She rang Kerry, hoping they could meet for lunch and have a few laughs. No cheer there. Kerry was distracted and upset because Trevor had received his call-up papers weeks ago and burned them.

"What are you going to do?"

"Look, Caro, I can't talk now, the walls have ears around here. Can you meet me for lunch at Smokey Jack's, about one o'clock?

"All right, I'll be there."

Caroline rang the hospital and found out the visiting

hours—two to four or six to eight, now that Mr. Harrington had been shifted out of Intensive Care. After meeting Kerry she would visit him, if Iris wasn't there. With any luck, the old witch would be attending some society function.

Iris would want to go at the same time as Bryce, to inject a little more venom into him. How could a mother cold-bloodedly plot the demise of her son's marriage? It was incomprehensible, downright evil.

At Smokey Jack's Caroline and Kerry hugged each other. "What's it like, being an old married woman?"

"Good, until yesterday, that is." She told her friend what happened.

"Evil old bitch. Bryce should have stood up for you."

"I know. He got upset about his father, but he should have supported me, or at least our baby. I'm frightened." She grasped her friend's hand. "Iris is going to plot and plan my downfall. Every single chance she gets, she'll sink the boots into me. Her one mission in life will be to turn Bryce against me."

"He's a selfish, thoughtless pig, but if you want him, you'll have to fight for him."

"What can I do?"

"I'd say you've made a good start." Kerry stared at her neck and Caroline blushed when she realized her friend had noticed the love bite. "Food and sex."

"Kerry!"

"It's true. Nice food and plenty of hot sex is the way to any man's heart. They're the only weapons you've got, so use them."

Caroline laughed. "You're incorrigible. How are things going with Trev?"

"Terrible." Kerry's grin disappeared. "The federal police came to his house on Sunday. If he doesn't report to the recruitment place on Thursday, they're going to arrest him."

"Oh, no! What are you going to do?"

"I'm not sure. We're going to an anti-conscription rally tonight. They're forming an underground network to help draft dodgers get away."

"The authorities will hunt him down."

"I know, but he refuses to go. It's not that he's a

coward. He just doesn't believe in the Vietnam war. He's a conscientious objector, but how can he prove it?" Her eyes darkened with bitterness. "If he were rich he could buy his way out, or stay at university until the war ends."

"It's not the army. It's the government. Andy says the soldiers don't want to fight with conscripts."

"Have you heard from him?"

"No, but he's going to Vietnam within the next couple of days. He told me on Saturday."

"I'm sorry. We're a miserable pair of sad sacks, aren't we?" Kerry downed her coffee in a couple of gulps. "I'd better get back to work." She squeezed Caroline's hand. "If Trev goes on the run, I'll be with him."

"You can't." Caroline's heart dropped to her boots. "It's madness."

"I have to. I love him. You can understand that, the way you feel about Mr. High-and-Mighty. I mean, you'd do anything for him."

She couldn't deny it. She would travel to the ends of the earth with Bryce.

Chapter 17

Caroline caught a cab to the hospital and was shown into Alexander's private room.

"How are you feeling?" She went over to the bed and kissed the old man's cheek.

"I'm all right. I can't stand all this fuss."

"I'm sorry about what I said on Sunday. I was a guest in your home."

"Don't worry about it. Iris can be vindictive if she gets a set on you."

"I think she hates me."

He chuckled. "She's no match for you, my dear. You're like your father; he wasn't afraid to stick up for himself."

"I acted badly, and I'm sorry. I was having such a good time before, with the photos and everything."

"I enjoyed the trip down memory lane, too." He patted her hand.

"You're such a nice, warm man, and your wife is..." Caroline tailed off. "I'm sorry."

"It's all right. Iris is cold, been that way for years, but she's not a bad woman. She gets fixated on things, and it impairs her judgment. Bryce and I have learned not to argue with her—it's easier that way. Ashley Fontain and Bryce together would be a disaster. It's as plain as the nose on your face, but Iris won't have it. Give her time, and she'll see the light."

Caroline didn't think such a bitter, twisted woman would ever change. Then again, she was a mother fighting for her son. Now, that Caroline could understand, sympathize with, even. She would kill to protect her child from danger.

"Now, my dear, what's happening in the outside world?"

"Not much. There's going to be an antiwar sit-in at the university on Friday."

"Feral, unwashed hippies. Round them all up," Alexander growled. "Put them in the army. It might make men out of them."

Thank goodness she hadn't mentioned Trevor's dilemma to him. Bryce would be equally unsympathetic. Born to money and privilege, conscription wouldn't worry them. They could buy their way out of it. Only a poor man's son ended up as cannon fodder.

She helped Alexander finish a crossword puzzle, and it was after three o'clock by the time she decided to leave.

"You don't have to scurry away." He chuckled. "Iris is coming in with Bryce after he finishes work."

"I didn't mean to be so transparent." Caroline laughed.

"I'll be going home tomorrow or the next day. Iris has arranged for us to spend a few weeks with friends at their Portsea beach house."

"Sounds nice."

"It overlooks the ocean. Clive has heart problems like me. Us old goats will have a few rounds of golf. The women will hit the chicken-and-champagne trail, and the charity tennis tournaments."

Caroline didn't want to return to Bryce's cold, sterile apartment. If she lived there for any length of time, she would have to brighten it up somehow. Passing a florist shop, she impulsively bought two large bunches of red and yellow roses.

She loved Bryce and would fight to win his love by following Kerry's advice. She was a good cook, the sex between them had been hot, and she would turn his stark apartment into a warm, inviting home.

****

Over the next couple of weeks, Caroline put her plans into operation. After buying a couple of recipe books, she asked Bryce's housekeeper to help her prepare some delicious meals. She got colorful cushions and scattered them over the couch and armchairs, bought pretty country-scene paintings for the walls, and put vases of fragrant flowers in the kitchen and lounge room.

It was no hardship decorating a place, with plenty of money to spend. Not cash money, but Bryce had set up accounts for her at several exclusive department stores.

When he arrived home each evening she welcomed him with a kiss, poured him out a cold beer and handed him the newspaper so he could read it before dinner.

In bed, she went to him eagerly, happily. The sex was steamy hot, mind-blowing. He was an excellent teacher, she an apt, ardent pupil. It took a few days for it to dawn on Caroline. Bryce never made love to her. It was sex, pure and simple. She didn't know how she could tell the difference, but she could. Not once, even at the height of his passion, did he ever say he loved her—because he didn't.

One afternoon she received a frantic call from Kerry. "Calm down! I can't understand what you're saying."

Kerry started crying and talking at the same time. "Trevor, the police."

"What!"

"The federal police have arrested Trevor."

"Why?"

"He refused to go to the army. I told you he's a conscientious objector. He escaped, but I need two thousand dollars to get him out of Australia. I don't know anyone with that kind of money except you."

"I haven't got much money."

"Harrington has. It would be chicken feed for him. Borrow some. I'll pay it back, I swear."

"Bryce wouldn't give me that much money."

"Oh, God," Kerry wailed. "Ten years in a military prison if he's caught. You said Harrington lets you buy whatever you like."

"He doesn't give me money. He just set up accounts at a couple of stores."

"Trevor's parents haven't got any spare cash, and my parents won't help. Dad would hand him over to the authorities. You're my last hope," she finished off on a sob.

"Maybe I could buy something worth two thousand dollars and return it the next day for a refund. Where are you now?"

"At our apartment in Prahran. The lease doesn't expire until the end of the month. Trevor's in hiding. There are a dozen draft dodgers sheltering in a couple of safe houses, but the federal police are closing in. I think they've been watching this place, so meet me tomorrow at Smokey Jack's with the money, okay? Thanks, I'll never forget this."

She didn't want to get involved in this kind of thing, but Kerry was her best friend. Two thousand dollars was a veritable fortune, she thought frantically. What could she buy that would cost two thousand dollars? A diamond ring or a bracelet? She could say they didn't fit after she got them home, and ask for a refund. Would they give her cash? More probably they'd just reinstate it on the account.

There must be a better way. She didn't have a criminal mind and wasn't very brave, but she had to come up with something. Ten years in prison to a young man like Trevor might as well be life.

If she bought jewelry, she could hock it at a pawnbroker. It was the only idea she could come up with.

She paced the floor. Bryce was her husband, and she had proved herself a good wife. Surely it wouldn't be unreasonable to ask him for money to buy maternity clothes and baby goods. He might fall for that.

Sheer willpower and the desperate desire to help Kerry wasn't enough to allow her to prepare the filet mignon and scalloped potatoes she had planned to have for dinner. Her head ached, her stomach started churning, and she desperately wanted to cry.

She lay down on the couch. A few minutes' rest might help her think of a better plan.

When Caroline woke up, she was shocked. "Five o'clock?" she shrieked, leaping off the couch. She could turn some leftover veal casserole into a curry. On a bed of rice it would look okay. Tinned fruit and ice cream for dessert? A pitiful menu, to be honest, but she had neither the time nor the energy to do anything else.

Bryce arrived home, hot and bothered and in a foul mood.

"Did you have a bad day?"

His quick, disinterested kiss skimmed across her mouth and landed on her cheek.

"An absolute shocker." He struggled to loosen his tie and collar and she did it for him. "What have you been doing with yourself? You look terrible."

"I've been feeling a bit nauseous and I've got a head..."

"See a doctor if you're not well. I'm going to take a shower. I've got to go to Canberra tonight."

"What!"

"The big army contract we tendered for—there have been problems with it. If I don't front up to some special tendering board tomorrow and talk things through, we're out of the race." He stalked off.

Caroline heated up some frozen bread rolls and put them in a basket, then surveyed the table to make sure it was set up nicely. When she heard Bryce moving around the bedroom, she spooned the rice into a pretty bowl and lifted the casserole out of the oven.

"What's that I smell?" he said, striding into the kitchen.

"Curry."

"Curry! I hate curry." He peered into the casserole dish. "I'm not eating curried leftovers."

"There's nothing wrong with it."

"Your job is to provide me with decent meals."

"Job! I'm not on your payroll. I'm your wife."

"You cost more than my employees," he shot back.

"And you don't think you're getting value for money?"

He picked up a roll, grimaced with distaste and dropped it back into the basket.

"You inconsiderate pig!" She knew she sounded like a fishwife but couldn't help it.

The breath hissed from between his teeth.

"I've done everything to try and please you, and you're never satisfied."

"Don't nag me. I'm not in the mood for it. I've had a hell of a day."

"And I haven't? I've been nauseous. I've got a headache and the zip on my favorite jeans won't do up anymore."

"Buy some new ones."

Inadvertently he gave her the opening she needed. She took several deep breaths to control her temper. "Could I have two thousand dollars?"

"What!"

"I need maternity clothes and things for the baby."

"Use the accounts I've opened up for you."

"But, but, I want to go to different shops."

"I'll sort something out when I get back. I'm sorry about before." He rummaged his fingers through his hair. "I really do hate curry. I'll grab something to eat at the airport." He went over to the phone and called a cab.

She went up to him and put her arms around his neck. "How long will you be away?"

"Two days, three, maybe. I'm not sure."

"It's too long to be on your own."

"You don't trust me. Think I can't survive without sex?" Angry color suffused his cheeks. "I haven't been on starvation rations lately."

The thought that he might turn to another woman almost killed her. "No, I give it to you every night." Why did he feel the need to ride roughshod over her feelings all the time?

He grabbed his overnight bag and stalked out of the room, and she could almost believe he was upset because she didn't trust him. She dashed to the door to call him back. Too late. He was gone.

Feeling about a hundred years old, Caroline cleaned away the uneaten meal. She ran herself a nice warm bath and soaked in it for half an hour before sadly trouping off to bed.

Next morning Caroline was up early. She couldn't let an argument with Bryce prevent her from helping Kerry and Trevor. After tidying up the apartment, she caught the elevator downstairs. In pale pink-and-white-checked slacks and a simple white button-down-the-front blouse she wouldn't stand out in a crowd.

She bought a solitaire diamond ring and matching eternity ring at one store, a chunky gold bracelet and a diamond brooch at another, knowing full well the pawnbroker would drive a hard bargain. She pawned the rings first. "They're worth much more than this. Look I've got the receipt."

"Listen, lady, it's only worth eight hundred bucks to me. Take it or leave it." She took it. She didn't have the luxury of telling this predatory shark how despicable he was, playing on people's desperation.

At the second pawnbroker's, she didn't fare much

better. "I'm sorry, things have been a bit rough lately," the man almost apologized. "If you could wait a couple of weeks, I might be able to give you more."

"I can't wait. I need the money now."

All up, she raised two thousand, three hundred dollars. She gripped her bag tightly. What if she got mugged?

When they met, Caroline couldn't hide her shock. White-faced, eyes red-rimmed from crying, Kerry was more distraught than Caroline had ever seen her.

"Thank God, you came. Have you got the money?"

"Yes, two thousand, three hundred dollars." She explained how she came by it.

"Daylight robbery. Money-hungry sharks." Kerry displayed some of her old fire.

They ordered cappuccinos and a piece of carrot cake.

"You might as well take all the money. You might need it."

"Thanks, but two thousand is enough. I'll never forget what you've done for us," Kerry said. "Never."

"It's the least I can do for a friend."

"Don't look now, but isn't that guy over there, the one in the navy shorts, staring at us?"

"I don't know." Caroline glanced around, as if casually observing a passerby.

"I think I've been followed." Kerry burst out laughing, as if she didn't have a trouble in the world.

Caroline forced a smile and tossed her head, pretending to ogle a young man sitting at a nearby table. Her mouth dried up. Butterflies twirled around in her stomach. She clasped her hands under the table so no one would see them shaking.

"What are you going to do?"

"I don't know." Kerry gave a hunted look around. "We'd better separate. You take the money to Trevor."

"What!"

"Pretend to give me some money. Make sure he sees. He'll follow me, and you'll go to Trev. I'll tell you where he's hiding."

"My God! What are you getting me into?"

"Caro, Trev's looking at ten years rotting in some military prison because he's standing up for his beliefs."

"I know, I know. It's just that Bryce would kill me if he ever found out. Andy, too."

"Yeah, Harrington would, but not Andy. He's fighting for what he believes in, like Trevor is. They're just on opposite sides."

Caroline found an empty envelope in her bag and made a big display of handing it over to Kerry.

"I'll dash off like I'm in a hurry and catch a train to Ringwood or somewhere, to lead him away," Kerry said. "You dawdle around, window shop for a bit, then catch the bus to the address in Carlton."

"All right. Good luck."

"Yeah, thanks. If you see Trevor, tell him I'll catch up with him tonight." Kerry scuttled off.

Caroline got up from her chair slowly. She wasn't very good at this cloak-and-dagger stuff. She wandered around the shops for a time, bought an ice cream and forced herself to eat it as she walked along. Finally, she deemed it safe to catch a bus to the address in Carlton.

It turned out to be a rundown double-storied place in a line of terraces. Shaking with nerves, she knocked on the door and waited. A bearded young man wearing a gray caftan opened it warily.

"Is Trevor Higginbotham here?"

"Who wants to know?"

"I'm Caroline Harrington, a friend of Kerry and Trevor."

"Trevor," he yelled down the passageway. "You know Caroline?"

The young man opened the door fully, and Caroline scuttled in. *Make love not war. No conscripts for Vietnam.* The walls were plastered with antiwar posters and peace signs.

Trevor, looking pale and drawn, gave her a hug.

"Where's Kerry?"

"She thought someone followed her, so she caught a train to Ringwood. She said she'll catch up with you tonight. I've got the money."

"Thanks. We'll pay you back one day, I swear."

"It's all right. Here's the money. Best of luck."

"Thanks. How's Andy?"

"All right. He's in Vietnam, I think, but I haven't

heard from him."

"Kerry told me he'd gone."

"Would you like a coffee?" Trevor asked.

"No, thanks, I'd better go. I'm no good at this cloak-and-dagger business."

"It's terrible. We're supposed to live in a democracy," he went on bitterly. "I'm not a coward. I would fight if someone attacked Australia, but this war is morally wrong. It's purely political." His mouth twisted. "I'm a fugitive in my own country, now."

"Don't get bitter. What are you going to do?"

"We've linked up with other antiwar groups. We're going to get out of Australia and lie low in a sympathetic country. Some American draft dodgers are crossing the border into Canada, but that's a bit far for us. I didn't want to involve Kerry in this, but you know what she's like. I love her, but I can't go against my conscience."

"I know, and a team of wild horses wouldn't hold Kerry back once she makes up her mind. I'd better go. Good luck."

"Thanks. When we get settled somewhere, we'll write. Might have to be a bit cryptic, though."

"Mention my dog Sebastian." She gave a nervous laugh. "Then I'll know it's from you."

Caroline caught the tram home, and by the time she let herself into the apartment she felt exhausted. *You're not cut out for all this clandestine stuff, my girl.* Why wasn't she going into screaming hysterics?

She couldn't be bothered cooking anything much for tea, so she heated up a little curried veal and ate it.

Would Bryce ring up to make sure she was all right, after the harsh words they'd exchanged? Not likely. What made him tick? Was he a chip off the old block? Alexander Harrington seemed a nice old man, but she suddenly recalled hearing office gossip about him having a ten-year affair with some woman in the accounts department. Could infidelity be in the Harrington genes? Iris might have been prepared to share her husband, but it had turned her into a bitter woman.

"I won't make the same mistake," Caroline vowed outloud.

Chapter 18

Caroline again woke early the next morning, revived after a good night's sleep. Her good deed must have tired her out. She wasn't sorry about helping Kerry and Trevor. That's what friends were for.

She showered and dressed, then cooked herself some poached eggs for breakfast.

The door buzzer interrupted her solitude. For some reason she glanced at her watch. Nine o'clock.

"I'm coming." She swung the door open. "Good..." The greeting died on her lips.

An army officer and a soldier stood there, somber-faced.

"Andy," she screamed. A black veil came down over her eyes. Her legs buckled and the officer sprang forward and caught her before she hit the ground.

"Your brother's all right." He helped her into the lounge room.

"He isn't dead? Hasn't been killed?"

"No, no. He's wounded, but it's not life-threatening. I'm Lieutenant Curtis."

"Sergeant James."

"Oh, God, I thought..."

"Where's your husband, Mrs. Harrington?"

"In Canberra."

"Make her a cup of tea, Sergeant—unless you want something stronger, um, Caroline?"

"No, tea will do. What's wrong with Andy?" She couldn't stop shaking. Her teeth were chattering and she felt icy cold. He wasn't dead. Thank God. He wasn't dead.

"He's sustained serious leg injuries."

"How serious?"

"Bad enough to get him out of Vietnam."

"He's coming home?"

"Yes, he and several others are being evacuated to the Heidelberg Military Hospital. There's a top orthopedic surgeon there."

"He won't lose his leg?" Visions of Andy hobbling around on an artificial limb brought tears to her eyes.

"I don't think so," the lieutenant said. "We haven't got many details. He'll be admitted to Heidelberg within the next couple of days."

Caroline trembled so much she had trouble holding the mug when the sergeant gave it to her.

"Thanks. Have one yourself."

"Is there someone who can stay with you?"

"No. My husband is in Canberra on business, some tender for the army. Ironic, isn't it?"

"Where's he staying? We'll ring him up for you."

"Thanks. I'm not sure where he is. What's the best hotel there?"

"The Grand," the lieutenant said. "Frightfully expensive."

"That's where he'll be. The Harringtons accept nothing but the best."

The lieutenant went over to the phone and got the operator to put him through to the Grand Hotel.

"Good morning. I'd like to speak to Bryce Harrington urgently. Put me through to his room, please. Thank you. Hello? Hello, is that Bryce Harrington's room?" he asked. "And you are? Ashley who?"

Caroline's heart turned to stone. Nine o'clock in the morning and Ashley Fontain answered the phone in Bryce's room.

"Where's Harrington?" the lieutenant snapped. "In the shower?"

"Hang up, hang up," Caroline pleaded, and the lieutenant dropped the receiver as if it were contaminated.

"What a bastard. I'm sorry, I mean…"

"It's all right." She felt calm, dead calm because her heart had frozen over. "I'm not surprised. I suspected he might have another woman." But not so soon. The ink was barely dry on their marriage certificate.

"Is there a hotel near the military hospital?"

"There's one around the corner," the lieutenant said.

"Could you ring and see if they've got a vacancy? I'll stay there until I find out what's happening with Andy."

"Sorry about all this." The lieutenant looked embarrassed, and the sergeant stood stony-faced.

"Don't be, I've been more or less expecting it. If the hotel has a vacancy, I'll stay four days initially." That three hundred dollars Kerry wouldn't take could prove to be a lifesaver. "Would you mind driving me over?"

"Of course not." The lieutenant picked up the phone again.

Hurriedly she packed a case, making sure to take only her own things. Anything that had been paid for by Bryce she left behind. Gold digger, was she?

All the store cards, the jewelry, and the keys to the apartment she piled in a heap on the island bar. She tried to slip her wedding ring off but her finger was too swollen. She must be suffering fluid retention. No wonder her legs felt puffy and tight.

She debated about leaving a note. If Bryce suspected foul play he would contact the police. And that she didn't want. Quietly, unobtrusively, she wanted to disappear from his life. Let him have the oh-so-suitable Ashley.

"Are you sure you're all right?" the lieutenant asked, staring intently at her.

"Yes," she said in a low, dead-sounding voice. There were no tears. The pain and humiliation went too deep. Bryce cared so little for her or their child that he could break their marriage vows without a twinge of remorse.

Something had died inside her. Only the thought of Andy, on his way home from Vietnam in God alone knew what condition, stopped her from collapsing in a heap on the floor. She was being dragged through the corridors of hell today.

She wrote a brief note. *Goodbye, Bryce. I hope you find the happiness with Ashley that you couldn't find with me. Caroline.*

"I'm ready to go now."

The lieutenant gave her a strange look. *Probably thinks I'm a cold-hearted bitch because I'm not screaming. If only he knew.* The pain of betrayal was so deep, so excruciating, her brain had instinctively switched into survival mode.

The sergeant picked up her case, and they left the apartment, leaving her dreams blown to smithereens and a cavernous hole in her heart.

****

Bryce loosened the collar of his shirt as he fumbled with the apartment door key. It was so late Caroline would be in bed. He should have waited and caught an early morning flight home, but he wanted to see her. He was desperate to take her in his arms and spend the night making wild, passionate love. God, he couldn't believe how much he had missed her, how much he needed her.

Next time he went away, he would take her with him. He opened the door and switched on the light. Like a slap in the face, the coldness assaulted him. The place felt as if all the warmth had been sucked out of it. A sudden feeling of foreboding slammed into him with the force of an out-of-control locomotive.

The place looked immaculate, as always. There were no flowers. He dropped his bag on the floor and dashed into the bedroom. Empty.

His mouth dried up and his stomach muscles clenched as he rushed into every room searching for signs of life. He found none. His apartment was cold, sterile, dead, because Caroline wasn't in it.

Was she sick? Met with an accident? He dashed back out into the kitchen, skidding to a halt on seeing the store cards, the keys and jewelry. Snatching up the note in trembling hands, he read it. Brief, to the point.

Bloody Ashley had presented herself at his hotel room at eight-thirty in the morning. He'd heard the phone ring as he stepped out of the shower. *Wrong number,* she had called out. It must have been Caroline. Naturally she would think the worst. Who could blame her?

He prowled up and down, still holding the note. Where would she go? He lit a cigarette and inhaled the smoke, trying to get himself under control.

Her old apartment was the only place he could think of. Even though it was late, he dialed the number.

"Who is this," a male voice said.

"Bryce Harrington. Who the hell are you?"

"Steven Branson, Federal Police."

"Federal Police?"

"Yes."

Bryce started to get a sick feeling in his gut. Kerry

was a shrew, a raving bloody lunatic, but not criminal.

"I've just come back from a business trip. My wife isn't here, so I thought she might be staying with Kerry. They used to share the apartment."

"We're interested in speaking to your wife, too. Where is she?"

"How the hell do I know? That's why I'm ringing." What was wrong with these people? "Do you know who I am?" Bryce snarled. "The Harrington name carries weight. I'll have your job for this."

"I don't think so. We have evidence that your wife is mixed up with hiding draft dodgers."

"What are you raving about? Caroline wouldn't have anything to do with those peaceniks."

"Trevor Higginbotham burned his call-up papers and refused to present himself for induction into the army. There's a warrant out for his arrest."

"What's that got to do with Caroline?"

"Does your wife have shoulder-length, streaky blonde hair? Slim build?"

Bryce gripped the phone to stop his hand from shaking. "What if she does?"

"She's been helping them."

"Rubbish! Her brother is in Vietnam with the army."

"She met up with Kerry and we followed her to a safe house in Carlton, a known haunt of draft dodgers. By the time we raided the place, they'd all gone."

"Caroline wouldn't be involved. She left me because we had an argument."

"You don't mind us searching your home, checking your phone records?"

"Yes, I damn well do."

"If your wife is innocent, as you claim, you should be anxious to prove it."

"All right." Bryce reluctantly agreed. Maybe if they could trace the phone calls it would help him find her. He felt desperate enough to try anything. He gave them his address.

"You don't think she's in any danger, do you?"

"Who knows?" Branson sounded as if he couldn't care less about Caroline's welfare. "They're ruthless, some of these people. Fanatics have infiltrated some of the antiwar groups. There's an underground escape route we want to find out about. This kind of treasonous behavior can't be tolerated."

"Don't preach to me. Caroline's father was a highly decorated soldier who was killed in the Second World War. Her brother is a serving officer, and she's as patriotic as any of us." Even as he defended her, the doubts crept in. Kerry and Caroline were close friends. Angry, upset with him, maybe she... He couldn't believe she would betray her country on purpose, but if she got mixed up with those creeps...

"Tomorrow morning, early," Bryce said.

"Okay, we should have the phone records by then. You can tell us if you know any of the people she called."

"All right."

Bryce gave him the information he wanted and hung up. He prowled around the apartment. Caroline had taken nothing that he gave her. So much for his mother accusing her of being a gold digger.

He should have stuck up for her that Sunday. He had been shocked by his mother's vitriol and hadn't wanted to exacerbate the situation. He knew from past experience how vicious she could be if she set her mind to it. When his father collapsed, he was too worried to think of anything else.

He poured himself a whiskey and stared broodingly into the glass as he slumped in an armchair. What if he couldn't find her? The place seemed empty now, cold as a mausoleum. She had turned his apartment into a home, something he'd never had before.

Why the hell hadn't he realized? The old saying about you didn't miss something until you lost it, well, that couldn't be truer. God, what if he didn't get her back? Worse still, if he couldn't find her? He stood to lose not only his wife but his child.

He hadn't treated her well. She was warm, generous, had done everything to please him, and what had he done for her? Thrown some jewelry and credit cards at her, snapped and snarled. God, he'd acted like some tin pot dictator.

She had been hurt, upset by his mother's treatment, and he had done nothing about it. He couldn't understand his mother, deliberately trying to wreck his marriage. Telling Ashley where he always stayed in Canberra, encouraging her to go up there and throw herself at him. It might have worked once—forbidden fruit had always attracted him, before.

He swallowed the rest of his drink and reached for the bottle. But, hell, getting drunk wasn't going to help. He went to bed, purely and simply because he didn't know what else to do.

****

Branson, of the Federal Police, arrived at the apartment right on nine o'clock.

"We've got the records for the last couple of months," he said without preamble. Bryce realized most of the calls were his. There was one to his Canberra hotel. So it *had* been Caroline who rang when Ashley answered it. The other number was in Heidelberg.

"It's a hotel," Branson said.

Caroline must have booked herself into it, but why Heidelberg?

"I rang them. She's there. I'm going over to arrest her."

"I'm coming with you." Wild horses wouldn't have kept him away. He didn't trust Branson not to bully Caroline into admitting to some trumped-up charge.

He didn't tell the policeman about the receipts from the pawnbroker, either. Caroline had gone to a pawnbroker to get the two thousand dollars he had refused to give her. What would she want that kind of money for? Had she been planning to leave him all along? His stomach plunged. Did she get it for Kerry, or some criminal? He couldn't decide which of the horrible scenarios he preferred.

"Will you take her back?" Branson broke into his brooding after they had been driving for about twenty minutes.

"She probably won't want to come back."

Branson gave a harsh bark of laughter. "Aiding and abetting a fugitive is a serious matter. She'll be desperate to use the Harrington money and name to save her neck."

Bryce ignored him.

The hotel turned out to be a clutch of single-storied

units set around a concrete square.

"Doesn't look much." Branson parked the car a little way up the street. "I don't want to scare her off."

"She's not an axe murderer," Bryce snapped.

Branson led the way to reception, where a woman sat smoking a cigarette. "We know Caroline Harrington is staying here. What room is she in?"

"She isn't here at the moment." The woman blew out a cloud of cigarette smoke. "She's gone to the hospital."

"Hospital!" What would she be doing in hospital? Oh God, the baby. Bryce felt his heart lurch, and a sick feeling curdled his stomach. "What's wrong with her?" he asked frantically.

"Nothing. She's gone to the military hospital."

"Military hospital?" Branson exclaimed. "Why the hell would she go to a..."

"To visit her..."

"Brother." Bryce cut the receptionist off. He felt as if a battering ram had slammed into his stomach. "Is he badly hurt?" Oh, God, Andy was only a boy.

"I don't know. The army contacted her this morning, saying he'd been admitted last night. She went over straight away."

"Where's the hospital?" Bryce asked.

"Around the corner. That sprawling blue-gray place."

"Thanks." He strode towards the hospital.

"Hey, wait for me." Branson caught up with him. "I'll come with you."

"You want to arrest my wife for treason at the bedside of her wounded soldier brother?" The last twenty-four hours had been the worst of his life. How badly injured would Andy be? Missing a limb? Fighting for his life? He felt so helpless. Poor Caroline would be distraught. Frightened. Upset and alone because he'd failed to support her.

They entered the hospital, and a receptionist directed them to Andy's room.

"Hell," Branson exclaimed, as a nurse escorted them through a large ward. "They're so young."

Mere boys, most of them, Bryce thought, glancing at the occupants of the dozen or so beds they passed by. Another war. Another batch of wounded heroes.

"How is Captain Dennison?" he asked the nurse.

"He's seriously wounded, but it's not life-threatening. He's pretty heavily sedated. You'll have to speak to the surgeon when he comes in."

****

"Andy, it's Caroline." Her tears fell onto his face. "Wake up." She tapped his cheek with her finger. His skin was white as death, but it felt hot.

"Andy, please."

His eyelids fluttered open. "Caroline?" he whispered. "What are you doing here?"

"You look terrible." She stared at his legs. They were both in traction and encased in plaster from the knees down. "Are you in much pain?"

"No. I'm drugged to the eyeballs."

"What happened to you?"

"We were in a convoy. The truck in front of me triggered a mine. It blew them to smithereens and my truck ran off the road and hit a tree." Andy shuddered. "I remember being chucked up in the air. I woke up in an evac chopper with some medic telling me the bones in my legs were shattered."

Tears filled her eyes as she reached for his hand. It felt hot, clammy.

"I caught a few bits of shrapnel in other parts of my body. Nothing serious, though." He gave a strained grin. "I shouldn't be here."

"Oh, no!" A black mist swirled before her eyes and she started shaking.

"Not that. Shouldn't be *here*." He squeezed her hand. "Here in Heidelberg, I mean. Being evacuated so fast."

She nearly collapsed with relief. He was talking in riddles and her fuddled-up brain couldn't grasp what he was saying. He was badly injured but safe. Nothing else mattered.

"I'm just glad you're here." Her voice was so scratchy she hardly recognized it.

"A politician and a couple of other dignitaries in my truck were injured, and the government wanted to get them home as soon as their medical condition was stabilized." He grimaced. "Bad politics to arrange an emergency evacuation back to Australia and not have at least a couple of wounded soldiers on board."

"I don't care how you got here," she said fiercely.

"How are you feeling, Caro?" His voice was low now and he looked exhausted.

"Good." She felt like death warmed up, after a sleepless night.

"How's Harrington?"

"He's..."

"I'm fine." Caroline caught her breath as Bryce strode purposefully into Andy's line of vision. "Aren't I, darling?" He rested his hands on her shoulders.

What did he want? How did he find her so quickly? She wanted to slap his hands away. Never feel his touch again. Turn on him like some cornered beast. Tell him what she thought of his despicable behavior.

"We're both fine." He was an accomplished liar. Plenty of practise.

Andy looked so pale and sick, she had to keep up the charade of being happily married. Her suffering was nothing compared to what he must have endured.

"I'm tired," he whispered. "Stay with me until I fall asleep. Come back later this afternoon."

"I want to stay with you. I'll be here when you wake up."

"No. Take her home, Harrington. She's on the verge of collapse. Come back in the afternoon. I'll be more alert..."

"No."

"Please, Caro."

"Your brother is right. You need to rest, and so does he. I'll bring her back later."

Caroline suddenly became aware of the man standing a few feet away from Bryce. "Is he a doctor?"

"No. My name is Branson, I'm from the..."

"Shut up," Bryce snarled. "For Christ's sake, it can wait."

As soon as Andy fell asleep Caroline pushed Bryce's hand away.

"We need to talk," he said.

"There's nothing to say. You've hurt me for the last time."

"I can explain about Ashley, if you'll give me a

chance."

"I'm tired. I'm going back to my hotel room."

"We need to talk, Mrs. Harrington. There's a café back there." Branson took her by the arm and escorted her out of the ward.

She stopped dead in the corridor. "If Bryce wants a divorce, he can have it."

"Branson isn't a divorce lawyer. He's a Federal Police officer."

"What!" She couldn't understand what was happening. Her head was spinning so fast she couldn't think straight.

"Here we are," Branson said as they walked into the cafeteria. "Coffee all round. I'll put it on my expense account. Three coffees, love." He snapped his fingers at the girl behind the counter. When she made to argue, he drew out his badge. "Bring milk and sugar, too."

He chose a table well away from the other diners, and before they were even seated he started to speak.

"You could be in a lot of trouble, Mrs. Harrington."

"Why? I haven't done anything." She was feeling sicker by the minute.

"Do you deny helping a fugitive escape…"

"A fugitive?" She cut him off. "What are you raving about?"

"Your friend Kerry has been under surveillance for days. You met up with her, didn't you?"

"Yes, for lunch."

"Come on, we know you went to a house in Carlton."

"Caroline," Bryce interrupted. "Don't say any more until we speak to my lawyer."

"I didn't do anything. Kerry needed some money. She told me to take it to some house in Carlton and give it to Trevor, which I did. That's all I know. I swear it."

"What did they want the money for?"

"I'm not sure." Telling the truth was her best option. Kerry and Trevor had not been caught, so what did it matter now. "She said they needed to get away."

"Helping a draft dodger is a serious offence."

"He's a conscientious objector. I helped Kerry because she's my friend. What did you expect me to do? Refuse? They wanted to get out of Australia. I don't know how, when or anything about it. I gave Trevor the money and left. Take me to jail. I don't care. I have to see Andy again, to make sure he's all right, and then you can do what you like with me."

The girl bringing over their coffee interrupted them.

"Keep the change." Branson gave her a five-dollar note. "Now look here."

"No, you look here. Caroline's told you what happened. Haven't you got any compassion? You can see the state her brother is in. She's pregnant, on the verge of collapse, so I'm warning you—lay off."

Bryce thumped his hand on the table, making the crockery rattle. "We've got friends in high places. What are your superiors going to think when they find out you're persecuting a young pregnant woman whose seriously wounded brother has just been evacuated home from Vietnam? It's not her fault you botched up your raid and let those peaceniks escape. The papers will have a field day."

"All right, all right. I just wanted to find out what she knew," Branson blustered.

"Let's get out of here." Bryce pulled her to her feet. "We'll go home."

They left the coffee on the table without tasting so much as a mouthful.

"No, the hotel. I have to be near Andy. The hospital has that number. You go back to the apartment. I don't live there anymore."

"Please, I can explain about Ashley. My mother gave her the name of the hotel. I was getting ready to step into the shower when she waltzed in."

He ran his fingers through his hair. "As soon as I finished my shower, I told her to get out and stop wasting her time, regardless of what my mother insinuated. She must have answered the phone when you called. I heard it ring."

"It was the lieutenant the army sent over to tell me about Andy."

"Oh, my God, I'm so sorry. We'll talk about everything when we get back to your hotel." Bryce put his arm around her shoulders, and she left it there. She wasn't capable of walking without support right now.

Once they left the hospital grounds, Branson took his leave of them, saying, "I'll be off. I don't think we'll need to speak with you again, Mrs. Harrington."

"That's right. And don't come anywhere near her or you'll answer to me," Bryce threatened.

"I'm sorry about your brother. I hope he'll be all right."

"Thanks, so do I." Caroline felt too weary to do anything but let Bryce lead her away. What a horrible man. If the likes of him were chasing Trevor, he could expect little mercy if he got caught.

When they got back to the hotel, Bryce followed Caroline into her room. There was a built-in wardrobe, a dressing table and a bed, nothing else. He tried to hide his distaste at its shabbiness.

"Would you like me to get you a cup of tea?"

"No, thanks. I want to lie down. My head is splitting."

She was trembling, white as death, but so beautiful his breath caught in his throat. He couldn't let her go. He wanted her too badly. He loved her. For the first time he admitted it. He wanted Caroline as his wife. Wanted her to be the mother of his child. It could be good between them, but he had to convince her.

She went into the bathroom and returned within a few minutes wearing a nightgown. Not one of the sexy ones he'd paid for, but a simple white one embroidered with teddy bears. It made her look about sixteen.

He hovered uncertainly. He couldn't remember ever feeling so powerless.

"Caroline, please, I'm sorry. I should have told my mother to shut up when she insulted you, but I didn't want to make things worse. When Dad took that turn, I couldn't think of anything else but him. It wasn't his first heart attack. I thought he might die," he went on desperately.

Automatically, he turned the bedclothes back for her. She didn't speak, just stood trembling with tears rolling down her cheeks.

He didn't know why, but he noticed for the first time that her belly looked slightly rounded.

"You're starting to show," he blurted out before he could stop himself.

"Do you think so?" Her hand went to her stomach in a protective gesture that sent ripples of emotion through him.

"Darling, I'm so sorry," Bryce drew her into his arms. "Can you forgive me? I love you. I want our marriage to work, and it will if you give me a chance to make things up to you."

"Bryce, I..."

"Please, Caroline." She felt soft and warm. He inhaled her special perfume, the fragrance of the woman he loved, and it was heady stuff. Picking her up, he laid her on the bed and came down beside her.

She stiffened away from him when he tried to put his arms around her. "No."

"Yes. I just want to hold you, nothing more."

"Did you really mean it when you said you loved me?"

"Yes. Now and for always." He kissed her trembling lips, and his heart leapt when she responded. He wanted to make mad, passionate love to her, but now wasn't the time. She was too vulnerable. "Go to sleep, darling, and we'll talk some more when you've rested."

He held her until she fell asleep, then eased himself away from her and left the motel room. No point in having money and power if you didn't wield it.

It took three phone calls for him to find out Andy's condition. The news wasn't good, but it wasn't as bad as he'd thought it would be, thank God. Both legs were fractured—clean breaks, fortunately. It was the left ankle injury that would be the boy's ticket out of the army, though.

Bryce made his way back to the mean little hotel room. God, he was tired. He'd hardly slept a wink last night. He dragged off his clothes and slid into bed beside Caroline.

"Where have you been?" She rolled over to face him.

"I'm sorry if I woke you up, darling." He put his arms around her and held her close. "I wanted to find out how Andy was doing."

"You went to the hospital without me?" She pummeled his chest with her fists. "You had no right!"

"Hey, don't get upset. I spoke to some people on the phone, that's all."

"Why would they talk to you?" Her eyes filled with tears. "I'm his next of kin."

"I used the Harrington name, and it opened a few doors."

She tried to move away from him, but he tightened his grip on her. "Don't you want to know what I found out?"

"Yes. Oh, God, of course I do." What was wrong with her? "Is he going to be all right?"

Bryce told her what he had found out.

"The army won't want him any more?" Caroline held her breath waiting for his reply.

"No, darling, they won't."

Bryce's news was like having a ton-weight lifted from her back. For once she was glad of the Harrington money and influence. Would Andy be upset when he found out his military career was over? He must have seen some terrible things over there. No sane person would want to return to that kind of hell on earth.

"He'll need a few months of rehabilitation," Bryce said. "And the orthopedic surgeon thinks he'll always have a slight limp."

"I don't care. I'm just glad he's home. Will you be able to give him a job?" She ran her fingers down the side of his face.

"Yes, there will be plenty of opportunities for him in the business. He's a bright boy, and we're always looking for talented people. He'll have connections in the army, and as it looks like we're going to get those defense contracts, he could prove very useful."

"I didn't dream it? You really did say you loved me, Bryce?"

"Yes. Kiss me, Caroline. Tell me you still love me after the way I've behaved, the wretched things I've said and done." He punctuated the sentence with kisses.

"I love you, Bryce," she said simply. "I only ever wanted you to love me."

"I do. I love you more than life itself."

He kissed her again. It was the sweetest, most sensuous kiss they had ever shared. Her dreams had come true. He held her close, whispering endearments, but asked nothing else of her, and she loved him all the more because of it. Bryce loved her. She had waited, prayed for such a miracle to happen—now it finally had.

All her prayers had been answered.

Andy was home. Maybe he would never be quite the same as before he went away, but at least the jungles of Vietnam would not be his grave. She felt truly blessed.

A word about the author...

Margaret Tanner has been writing for as long as she can remember. She is a Medical Typist and lives in Melbourne, Australia, with her husband. She has three grown sons and one granddaughter. She is a history buff from way back. Her favorite period in history is the First World War, and she has in fact visited the battlefields of France and Belgium, and Gallipoli in Turkey, a poignant experience she will never forget.

Visit Margaret at www.margarettanner.com

Thank you for purchasing
this Wild Rose Press publication.
For other wonderful stories of romance,
please visit our on-line bookstore at
www.thewildrosepress.com.

For questions or more information,
contact us at info@thewildrosepress.com.

The Wild Rose Press
www.TheWildRosePress.com